ATOLL

A SEVEN SEAS ADVENTURE

KEITH DISSINGER

Keith Dissinger

V3

For Leanne,
Your support is immeasurable.

ATOLL, at-oll – noun. Reef, a ring shaped island or chain of islands formed of coral.

1

East coast of Florida 1970

The wind still howled, but with much less intensity. Now that the hurricane had moved up the coast, it was safe to go outside again. Ricardo Baez's shoulder-length black hair blew in the strong breeze as he walked along Daytona Beach. He wore no shoes, and only a T-shirt and cutoff shorts covered his lanky frame.

The September air blowing in off the ocean felt cool, almost cold. Spots of light began to break through the overcast sky. Ricardo felt glad to get back outside at last. Staying inside the school, hunkered down with his parents, had given the fifteen-year-old boy a sense of claustrophobia.

He walked the deserted beach and marveled at the changes the storm had made to the coast line. High dunes of sand were pushed up in rows along the beach. Assorted debris lay scattered around. Up ahead, he saw a whole tree lying on the beach. The storm must have torn it up from somewhere before depositing it here.

As he approached, he could see several different things

tangled in its branches. Ricardo saw plastic bags, a piece of tarp, even a mangled children's tricycle. A few cans and bottles were snagged by the heavier branches, while bits of cloth hung from the lighter branches.

Ricardo circled the tree poking at something here and there that looked interesting. He half-turned to continue along the beach, when something caught his eye. Something shiny stuck up from the sand. Ricardo knelt beside the object and began to dig. Soon, he had uncovered a metal object about the size of a large belt buckle. The object was shaped in a rectangle and Ricardo thought it might be made of brass.

Clearing the sand away, he could make out lettering on one side of the object. He took a piece of cloth from one of the branches and scrubbed harder. The storm wasn't entirely gone yet, as rain once again began to fall on the Daytona Beach area. Ricardo did not notice. He worked at the metal until finally he could read the lettering on the face. It spelled out *Captain*.

Ricardo believed he'd found something like a placard from the door of a ship. The feeling of elation that rushed through his body was unlike anything he'd ever experienced before. With a wide smile, he stared at the object for a long while. Finally, he placed it in his pocket and headed for home.

Over the next week, Ricardo visited the school library often to try to bring light to his discovery. He also spent countless hours combing the beach around his home in an attempt to find another treasure. He found many things, but they were all modern things washed into the sea by the storm. As for the placard, the only thing he found was a picture of a captain's stateroom door with the same type of placard. He had never told anyone of his discovery, preferring to keep the find to himself. After about a month, the excitement wore off. However, Ricardo's lust for discovery never faded.

———

Okefenokee Swamp Georgia 1976

"It's not here, friend," Juan Carrera announced in an authoritative tone.

"It is here," Ricardo replied. "It has to be here."

"Well you can keep looking, but I am done with this. It's time to drink beer and spend the last few days of summer relaxing," Juan said, throwing down his shovel. "I'll be in the truck."

If Ricardo noticed his friend's agitation, he did not let it show. He just kept digging. "I'll be there soon."

Juan took a few steps toward the truck, then stopped and said, "You know if it was here we would have found it by now, Ricardo?"

"I do not know that. I have done all the research. The robbers hid their loot here, right here."

"Yes, just like the last wild goose chase you dragged me along on, driving all the way to Alabama to find Civil war treasure. How about the time we rented a boat and snorkeled off that reef to find pirate treasure? It was fun for a while, but we have wasted far too much time and money on nonsense. You are my best friend Ricardo, but this treasure hunting is insane."

Ricardo's shovel hit something solid. He and Juan stared at each other for a moment. Even from where Juan stood twenty feet away, he heard the sound. He grabbed up his shovel and joined in with Ricardo digging frantically. Soon, they unearthed a metal box. Ricardo understood what he'd found and what it meant.

The legend said two men broke out of the Central State Prison in 1900. The men worked as janitors and house-keepers at the prison and the warden's apartment. Gaining the trust of the guards and warden, the inmates stole a safe from the warden's office rumored to hold the payroll for all the employees at the prison. The men overpowered two guards and made their escape into the swamp. The escapees were hunted down with hound dogs and captured a week after their escape. One man was shot and killed outright. The other man drifted in and out of consciousness for a month, losing his life at last.

Before he died, he told a story of burying the safe deep in the swamp. For years people searched for the safe without producing results. While the legend was still a popular topic of conversation among locals, most historians believed the prisoner gave incorrect information. Because of his delirious state, it was an easy explanation as to why the safe was never found.

Until now.

Ricardo and Juan worked their shovels fiendishly until they had the safe free. They hoisted the heavy, iron safe out of the ground and stared at it for a long while. For Ricardo, finding the safe was the culmination of intense searching and planning. He scoured the testimony of those involved. He went over every possible route the prisoners could have taken. He and Juan had spent the better part of their last two summer vacations from school plodding through the Georgia swamp.

Juan wanted to open the safe immediately. Ricardo wanted to be known for the discovery, not for the fame, but because he knew it could lead to other things. He might be able to secure a grant to go searching for something else. That was what he really wanted to come from his discovery . .. the opportunity to search for something else.

Since it was Ricardo's expedition to begin with, Juan had no choice but to go along with his idea. They took the safe to Georgia Southern University. Ricardo called the local newspaper to come and cover the story. He wanted the find to get as much exposure as possible.

With the help of University staff, the safe was opened. The rumors were true. The safe held just over seventy thousand dollars, a lot of money for 1900. The bills were moldy and not of much use now, other than for their historical value. Ricardo knew he'd made the right decision. The notoriety gained him the means to continue his ever-growing quest for discovery. Within six months, he was fully funded for another expedition, and another after that. For six years he explored, searching for one lost treasure or another. For six years he came up empty.

When the State funded academic money ran out, he sought for and found private funding. Ricardo moved on to bigger, better expeditions in exotic locales around the world. He had a particular interest in South America, mostly due to the belief that a good deal of treasure still waited to be found there. On his third expedition in 1987, he discovered a lost Incan village. It turned out to be the biggest find in that part of the world in fifty years. The find brought in more notoriety and more funding. For the next ten years, Ricardo Baez searched. He got to live out his dream, spending most of his time in South America. Ricardo made a few small finds, but nothing like the Inca village in 1987.

Society Islands 1997

He knew he was close. If the raft would just hold up, he'd make it. The small atoll lay no more than a mile away and the current was moving the raft in the right direction. Ricardo could barely believe he'd ended up in this position. When he'd followed a lead to the South Pacific, he thought it would be a welcome diversion from the dank jungles of South America.

Now, his life teetered on whether he could make landfall on a speck of land a mile away. He had set out with the most up-to-date equipment. His boat had all the comforts of home. He thought he had the resources to handle whatever minor situations would pop up. After all, warring native tribes were a thing of the past. The days of landing on islands and having to fight off cannibals were long gone. Or so he thought. However, three days after setting foot on the small island of Taurito, his entire crew was gone, killed by the crazy Chief of the Tauri tribe back where he'd just come from.

Ricardo had been lucky to escape. A young boy helped him by untying his hands, or he too would have met death in the fire. The other five members of his crew were one by one tied to a stake and burned alive. Ricardo did not know why the boy had saved him, but all he could do now was try to make it to the island and to safety.

The Chief and his tribe would not follow him here. They superstitiously thought the island was haunted. Supposedly, the ghost of a warrior protected the Oligand Tapu, an enormous treasure deposited by Spanish seafarers centuries ago. Anyone who set foot on the island would be killed by the warrior. The Oligand treasure is what brought Ricardo here in the first place. Through extensive talks with the tribal nobles, Ricardo had discovered the location of the treasure.

He had spent his life around superstitious native people and he wasn't about to let an age-old tale scare him off. He paddled the flimsy raft toward that atoll now. Besides, his life depended on making it to the atoll. With the wrath of the Chief bearing down on him, this was the only place he'd be safe.

Ricardo looked back. Far in the distance he saw four boats bouncing over the waves. The villagers finally found out he'd escaped, and they were coming after him. Unlike his handcrafted and hand powered raft, the villagers had motors on their fishing boats and it wouldn't be long until they caught up to him. His only hope was to make it to the small island before that happened.

Lying flat on his stomach on the raft of coconut trunks lashed together, he used his arms to paddle. The boy showed him to the raft and helped him push off from the beach. Ricardo had been lying on this raft, barely staying afloat since just before dawn. Bright sunlight reflected off the clear, blue surface of the water. He used one hand to shield his eyes as he checked the sun and estimated the time at noon. If only he could move faster.

The unwieldy raft proved to be hard to maneuver and Ricardo closed the distance to the island at an agonizing pace. Periodically, he would take a quick glance back. He didn't like what he saw. The boats were coming, gaining fast. He paddled harder, but knew he wouldn't make it. They were going to catch him.

In a desperate move, he flipped off the raft. Ricardo had grown up on the beaches of Florida and was a decent swimmer. He stroked hard for shore, now only one hundred yards away. In a few seconds, the boats were at the raft. They pulled up and Ricardo could hear a loud discussion taking place. He felt something solid slide by underneath his body as he swam. He was passing over a reef. The surf helped him along, pushing him toward the atoll, but once he made the inside of the reef where the bay was protected, there would be no surf. He'd have to swim in calm water. When that happened, Ricardo felt certain the boats would surely catch him.

Taking a quick glance back, Ricardo saw one of the three boats coming after him. The others stayed out away from shore. Ricardo guessed they were frightened to go close to the atoll. The one that did come, came on fast. In seconds it was on him. Three men were in the open fishing boat. The man in the bow held a long spear in his hands. As the boat closed the distance, he raised the spear. Just before he threw the seven-foot razor tipped spear, the boat hit the reef. The whole boat shuddered and sent men flying forward. The man with the spear flew out of the boat. The force of the impact was so great, he flew right over Ricardo's head. The spear went wild, never coming close to Ricardo. The other two men were also thrown from the boat.

The wooden boat's bow shattered. The motor revved before stopping when the operator was thrown overboard. Waves swamped the broken vessel and in less than ten seconds it went under. Two of the men struggled to swim out to the other boats. One man made it, the other had severe injuries. As he tried to swim to the boats, his head dipped under the waves and came back up several times before staying under for good.

Ricardo swam hard for the beach. He got ready for a fight when he swam past the man who had been thrown over his head, but when he got close, it was obvious the man was dead. Ricardo expected another boat to come up behind him at any moment, but when he stumbled up onto the sandy beach, he looked back and saw the boats still bobbing in the waves offshore.

Not stopping, he staggered into the dense forest and plopped down against a tree. Through the brush, he watched as the boats turned and headed back to the small island from where they had come. He knew they wouldn't come back. He had made it.

2

Present Day

An occasional white wispy cloud drifted past the steep mountains of Tahiti. Walter Ulrich marveled at the beauty of the island. While he'd visited some very nice locales, the island was unlike anything he'd ever experienced. Pristine, clear water and deep-green, lush forest assaulted the senses.

He had come to Tahiti to meet with Mitchell Hathaway. Mitch and his family were on assignment for Seven Seas Television and Walt worked as a field producer for the show. While he'd spoken to Mitch several times over the phone, and even Face Timed, he'd never met the Hathaways in person. He met with the family on their sailboat in Tahiti and resolved some issues they'd been having.

With the work finished he thought it was about time he got to relax and enjoy the South Pacific. Walt had planned on taking an extended vacation to the South Pacific after he'd discovered a lost Spanish treasure and lost a friend in the process, but when the opportunity to work as a producer came up, he jumped right in. Although he loved his job, he suddenly found himself in one harrowing situation after another.

Walt figured the first thing he should do is call and let his boss know he'd be out of the game for a while. As the thirty-eight-year-old leaned his six-foot, one-hundred-and-seventy-pound frame back in the wicker chair at his table in a sea side café, he couldn't stop a smile from forming. A vacation had been a long time coming. Walt was certain his boss, who was also the owner of the company, would understand. The two were close friends, and Walt had a feeling they'd become closer very soon.

"Hi, Barb, how are you?" Walt asked when the call went through.

"I'm terrific. How about yourself?"

Walt could feel her smile through the phone. He said, "I couldn't be better."

"Sounds as though Tahiti agrees with you."

"That it does. What a beautiful island."

"Hmm, sounds nice," Barb mused. "Did you meet the Hathaways?"

"I did. They are an awesome family. They fit right in with your team."

"Good, I'm glad to hear that coming from someone else. Art hired them. He and Mitch were buddies in the Marine Corps. I only ever spoke to them by phone and . . . while they seemed like a good fit, I couldn't really be sure."

"Well, you can be sure now. Both Mitch and Claire have good heads on their shoulders. Really, Barb, I'm impressed."

"That's great news."

"And those kids," Walt went on, "they'll steal your heart."

"Yea, I'm going to have to make time to get out in the field soon and meet them."

"Why don't you come down to Tahiti? We'll take a boat and meet up with them."

"Ha! I wish I could. I'm so swamped here I just can't get away." Barb's duties as CEO of the giant adventure company did not allow for many impromptu vacations. When her husband unexpectedly died, Barb stepped up and took over the reins. The athletic, former Adventure Racing athlete ran the company smoothly and with a solid efficiency. The Seven Seas television channel concept was in the prelaunch stage at the time of Art's death. Now, the channel enjoyed high rankings and was fast becoming a money-making machine.

"I thought you were going to hire an assistant?"

"I did," Barb replied, "remember, Martha?"

"You said you were thinking about her, but I didn't know you went ahead with it," Walt said in a surprised tone. "So, if you have an assistant, why are you still so busy?"

"Ask your pal Brock."

"What do you mean?"

Barb said, "They're on vacation together for two weeks. She's going to start when she gets back."

Walt's jaw dropped. "You're kidding."

Barb chuckled. While not the gossipy type, she enjoyed letting Walt in on the secret. "Nope. They're renting a cabin on a lake somewhere in the wilds of Minnesota."

"No. You're kidding. You've got to be pulling my leg."

Barb chuckled harder. She was really getting a kick out of Walt's reaction. "No. I'm serious. They hit it off right away I guess. They are both from the Midwest you know."

Walt paused for a moment to let it sink in. "I'll be damned," he said at last.

"Well, I'm happy for the two of them, and you should be too."

"Yea, I am, don't get me wrong. It's just hard to fathom after hearing Brock's big 'I'm a bachelor for life, no one woman can tie me down' talk over the years."

Laughing outright now, Barb said, "I know. It is funny, but I hope things work out for them."

"Me too," Walt said, also laughing. After a brief pause, he started on a new subject, "Speaking of vacations . . . I hope you don't mind if I take a couple of weeks off. I never did get that South Sea vacation I was planning."

Barb knew it was true. If anyone deserved a vacation, it was Walt. "No, I don't mind at all."

Walt thought he sensed something in her voice. "Are you sure, Barb?"

"No," she insisted. "You've certainly earned it. Riley Willets had a few days off when he got back from South Africa. He can cover while you're gone."

"Thanks. I am really looking forward to relaxing a bit." He hesitated while deciding. Finally, he said, "Why don't you come down, Barb? Tahiti is beautiful beyond words."

"I'd like to, Walt, I really would, but I'll have to pass. Next time?"

"Next time it is."

"OK, keep in touch, whether it's regarding work doesn't matter, I just want to hear from you."

"I will. The invitation's open if you change your mind. If not, I'll see you in about two weeks."

"See you in two weeks," Barb said, ending the call. Before she'd even set the smart phone down on her desk, she knew she was going to Tahiti. You could only fool yourself for so long.

3

Walt spent the rest of the day doing something he didn't normally do. He hung around the beachside bar and drank. Walt enjoyed a few beers once and a while, but he wasn't usually a big drinker. For the first day of his vacation, he thought he'd celebrate by enjoying the spectacular scenery while downing a few drinks. The bartender had a flare for making alluring Hurricanes that not only looked great, but also tasted delicious.

He allowed his mind to wander, but found himself thinking about his friends the most. His two closest friends, who he had gone through life and death situations with, were fading out of the picture. Denny Smith was married and expecting his first child soon. Brock McGowen was apparently dating and spending time with his new love on a remote lake somewhere.

After a few drinks, Walt decided to call Brock. The phone rang six times before it went to voice mail. When he listened to the greeting and waited for the beep, Walt left a message. "Hey, Brock, I heard you were running a trap line up north with a Native American or something like that.

Keep your lines tight and your powder dry and all that stuff. Anyway, I'm in Tahiti. I'm taking a vacation. I'll be here for about two weeks. Give me a call when you get back to civilization. Watch out for bears."

He swirled the little umbrella in his drink and reflected on some of the exploits he shared with Brock and Denny. However, soon his thoughts drifted to another friend. Barb Kendall, owner of Kendall Outdoors, the parent company of Seven Seas. Barb had been married to another of Walt's close friends, Art, who died saving Walt's life. Although he felt a pang of survivor's guilt, Walt felt his attraction to Barb growing by the day. He threw back his drink and ordered another. Walt walked over to the railing that surrounded the small bar. Leaning on the rail, he took in the sights. He marveled at the huts built on stilts out over the water. Although he chose to stay at a hotel within walking distance of the beach, Walt thought the huts would be an enjoyable place to relax.

The thought of sleeping directly over ocean water reminded him of the days when he vacationed with his best friends Brock McGowen and Denny Smith. The men always spent a night or two sleeping under the stars on the deck of their rented boat.

Every time he tried to focus on something different, his thoughts went back to Barb. Walt knew he'd have to do something about the situation. He and Barb had never flirted, but they passed small innuendoes back and forth for some time now. The last time he'd seen her, they'd shared a long kiss. Walt vowed to accept the fact that he was falling in love with Barb. He also vowed to tell her how he felt as soon as he returned to the United States. He smiled. For now, he was going to enjoy his vacation.

Walt felt a little hungover the next morning. He skipped

breakfast and went to the exercise room for a workout. He worked out with weights for twenty minutes, followed by twenty minutes on a treadmill. After working up a good sweat, he spent some time in the steam room. When the heat became too much, Walt hit the shower and headed for the pool.

By the time he strolled out to the pool area, Walt's hangover was gone. He set his personal items on a table by a lounger and went for a swim. A half hour later he laid back in the lounger for a nap. A smile creased his face as he began to truly relax.

The next few days drifted lazily by in the same manner, minus the hangover. Walt spent the days swimming in the pool, or the warm water of the South Pacific, and lounging on the white sand beach. He worked out daily just to keep his fitness edge. One day he went snorkeling but overall, Walt didn't really do much of anything . . . and he loved it.

By the fourth day Walt sported a deep, dark tan. He had just sat at a table on the patio of the hotel restaurant when his phone rang. He smiled when Barb's name showed up on the screen.

"Hello, Barb."

"Hi, Walt. How are you?"

"I'm doing great, you?"

"Better all the time. I've been meaning to ask, how is the food there?"

Walt thought that was a strange question. "The food's great. As a matter of fact, I just sat down to dinner."

"Do you have company?"

"No," Walt replied. "I'm fine with my own company."

"You wouldn't want anyone to join you for dinner then?"

Walt did not know what she was getting at, but he played along. "That would depend on who was joining me."

"I see," Barb teased. "If it was me, would you object?"

"Of course not. What are you talking about, Barb?"

"Turn around."

When Walt swiveled in his seat, a wave of astonishment washed over him as he saw Barb standing in the entrance of the restaurant. She wore a breezy red dress, had a bag slung over her shoulder, and held another in her hand. She held her phone to her ear, and a big smile on her face.

Walt dropped his phone. He stood, almost knocking the chair over, and rushed to Barb. She put her phone down and they fell into each other's arms. They didn't speak. Walt didn't have to ask what she was doing here. He knew.

After a long kiss, Barb said, "Are you going to help me check-in?"

Walt nodded. "I'll add you to my room."

Barb nodded in agreement.

Walt and Barb walked arm in arm to his room. They stayed in all night, foregoing dinner.

The next several days felt like a honeymoon. Walter Ulrich and Barb Kendall could not get enough of each other and did not want to be separated. Months of pent-up feelings, along with weeks of very stressful, sometimes life and death situations, melted away in the warm waters of the South Pacific and in each other's arms.

The third afternoon after Barb had arrived found her sitting next to Walt by the hotel pool. Like Walt, she wore swim clothes. The hotel provided Wi-Fi, so Barb talked on her phone and worked on her laptop at the same time. She'd been discussing business with several Kendall Outdoor employees.

Covering the mouthpiece of the phone with her hand, Barb said, "Sorry, Walt, I shouldn't be much longer."

Walt didn't mind. In all the time he'd known her, Barb had never spent much time away from her business and especially her phone. This was the first time since she'd been here, that he'd seen Barb even touch her phone. "That's fine. I understand," he said, smiling.

A half hour later when Barb finally ended her call, Walt asked, "Is everything all right?"

"Yes, the company is in good hands now that Martha Brown is on the job," Barb said with a chuckle.

"Brock and Martha are back from vacation?"

"Yes. Today's Martha's first day. She's working mostly from Minnesota, so the biggest challenge is getting all the communications set up. I find it amazing that once you have things set up right, and I don't know much about how that works, but you can do things from anywhere around the world."

"I agree with you; today's technology is amazing."

"As for Martha's business skills, I think she'll be fine. I'd rather have a loyal assistant, who works hard and cares, than someone who has a wall full of degrees."

"I agree with you on that too."

Barb giggled. "You're pretty agreeable today. Are you sure you're not trying to butter me up?"

"You're a smart woman, Barb. I happen to agree with your ideas."

"I must have something up here," she replied, pointing to her head. "Look who I found myself with."

Her reply sparked a question. Walt asked, "Did you have any idea this would happen? I mean we had been casual friends for a few years, but that's all. When we talked at

Denny and Lynne's wedding, did you think about us being together?"

"No. Absolutely not. That was too soon after Art's death."

"Right, the same goes for me. I never thought of you in this way," Walt paused. "I think you grew on me."

"You fell in love, you mean."

Walt raised an eyebrow.

"Go ahead, be a big tough guy, but you know it's true."

Walt let out a deep breath. "You're right. I am in love with you. The more time I spent around you and got to know you better, the more I wanted to be near you." When Walt finished, he looked at Barb.

She didn't gloat. She had a thoughtful look on her face. "I'm in love with you too, Walt."

Changing the subject, Walt held up a brochure. "Want to go for a helicopter ride around some of the islands?"

Barb let out a laugh. "Sure, but you're going to go broke if you keep this up."

"I might not own huge companies like you, Barb Kendall, but I am a millionaire don't forget." His statement was true. Although Walt did not pursue an extravagant lifestyle, he had become a millionaire when he discovered a long-lost Spanish treasure.

"Forget. Hell, why do you think I'm with you?"

Now it was Walt's turn to laugh. While it was true his net worth was over a million dollars, Barb Kendall's vast holdings made her a millionaire many times over. When her husband died, he had left her several homes, investment properties, and two major companies which each produced large six-figure revenues.

4

_____

Early the next morning, Walt and Barb had a taxi take them to the airport where the hangar for the helicopter company was located. They met the pilot, interviewed the man, and determined him to be qualified. No one wanted to go down in a helicopter crash this far out in the Pacific Ocean.

The ride around the island of Tahiti alone was worth the price of the trip. Dazzling mountains rose up from the blue waters in utter beauty. A squall in the distance gave the scene amazing contrast. Even Barb, who traveled the world as an adventure athlete in her younger days, was taken aback.

Tahiti was one of the Windward Islands that made up the Society Islands. The Society Islands supported one of the healthiest reef systems in the world. When the pilot flew out over the crystal clear ocean, the reefs were easily visible from the helicopter.

They flew over some of the smaller islands in the area. Many of these unnamed atolls were so small, they were not inhabited. In this part of the Pacific, the water's clarity revealed entire barrier reefs. Some of the reefs surrounded the atolls and provided calm, sheltered coves. Through the microphone in his helmet, Walt asked the pilot if he could circle a few of these islands.

Walt was a certified scuba diver and loved diving among the ocean's reefs. Growing up in New Jersey and living most of his life on the East Coast, he'd never had the chance to dive in the Pacific. After getting a close look at these undisturbed wonders of nature, he could hardly wait to get in and under the water. The water was so clear, the reefs were visible in stunning detail from the air.

Walt's head turned as if on a swivel as they flew low over one of the tiny atolls. "There's something down there," he said aloud.

Barb looked at him, shook her head, and mouthed the words, "What did you say?"

Walt keyed his mike and said, "I saw something down there along the reef." He got the pilot's attention and pointed. "Can you circle please? There's something down there along the reef."

The pilot nodded. He dropped in altitude and brought the chopper around in a slow circle.

"There," Walt said. "There's something in the reef."

The pilot didn't see what Walt pointed out, but he slowed and hovered over the place where Walt indicated he'd seen something.

"What do you see, Walt?" Barb asked. She didn't see anything either.

"I don't see it now, but I saw something right below us. Take us around again," he said to the pilot.

The pilot followed Walt's instruction. Twice he circled the spot Walt pointed out on the reef, and twice no one saw anything out of the ordinary. Walt however, knew he'd seen something on the first pass. He just didn't know what it was. At last, Walt instructed the pilot to continue with the tour. The flight lasted two hours and Walt and Barb relished the time flying over and around the atolls. The green foliage and white sand beaches of the many tiny, uninhabited coral atolls that dotted the ocean provided a stark contrast to the sparkling blue South Pacific waters.

When they returned, Barb wanted to visit one or two of the villages on the island. Tahiti was part of French Polynesia and the official language of the island was French. Walt and Barb hired a local who spoke English along with French to drive them around and tour the island. They spent the afternoon shopping and exploring the island. The small shops attracted Barb's full attention. She relished the idea of focusing on nothing but shopping. She felt no pressure, no stress of any kind. Most of all, she felt happy.

Walt did a bit of shopping himself. For him, the enjoyment came more from soaking up the local culture. Walt had always been fascinated by the volcanic and coral South Sea Archipelagos and the first adventurous Europeans who traveled to these far-off places. The island was a part of The Kingdom of Tahiti until it was annexed by France in 1880. He found it fascinating to imagine the first modern ships to discover the Society Islands hundreds of years ago. What must the island and her people have looked like at the time? He made a promise to himself to come back another time and do even more exploring.

As a rain squall passed over the island, Walt and Barb ducked into a small café for a bite to eat. Walt took a hard look at Barb. What he saw was a genuinely happy person. They sat close together at a table by the window drinking nonalcoholic, cool, fruity drinks.

"You don't mind spending most of the day alone on a deserted island?" Walt asked.

"I don't mind, but I'll worry about you diving."

"Oh, come on. This is me you're talking to, I'll be OK."

Barb glared at him.

"I won't take any chances, I promise."

The next day, Walt made plans for everything needed for his diving excursion. He could have done it when they returned from the helicopter ride, but there was no hurry. This vacation had a long way to go. Between phone calls and making arrangements, Walt relaxed on the beach with Barb. For her part, Barb spent about a half hour on the phone ensuring her business was running smoothly. Afterward, relaxation was the only thing on her mind.

The following morning, Walt and Barb used the same helicopter service as the day before. A delivery van brought the dive gear and an instructor to the hangar where the helicopter service was located. The instructor helped load the gear into the Enstrom Turbine 480B five-passenger helicopter. The dive instructor would go along just in case there was any trouble. Having an extra diver along seemed like a good policy.

Walt introduced himself then Barb to the instructor. His name was Pierre Hanleth. He had been an instructor for five years and he worked at one of the hotels before that. During the time they got to know one another better on the ride out to the atoll, Walt and Barb found Pierre an engaging guide. As a native of Tahiti, he had an intimate knowledge of the culture and history of the Society Islands.

Through headsets, Walt and Barb heard fables of island life long since gone. Pierre told stories of how families lived together in small groups. He touched on many aspects of ancient Polynesian life including the fishing culture and even religion. Along with the conversation, the sunny, post-card day made the ride more enjoyable.

When they approached the atoll that Walt had picked to dive, the pilot slowed and set the light-duty helicopter down on the narrow strip of sand beach. He killed the engine, so they could work without the noise. When the rotor stopped turning the blades, they all chipped in to unload the equipment.

With everything set out on the beach, the pilot fired the engine, lifted off, and flew away back toward Tahiti. Barb unfolded a light beach chair, peeled down to her swimsuit, and watched while Walt and Pierre prepped for the dive. Walt, like his guide, did not bother with a wet suit, preferring to wear swim trunks instead. When they were ready, Walt gave Barb an OK signal and waded into the sparkling clear water with Pierre trailing close behind.

Close to shore, the water remained calm. When the divers got out close to the reef, Walt felt the swirling action of the surf. The water felt like a cool draft as the men slipped below the surface. Kicking at a steady pace, they made their way out to where Walt thought he had seen something. They passed over the reef and for a while, the water was barely four feet deep. Abruptly, when they got to the ocean side of the reef, the bottom dropped away into deeper water that turned deeper shades of blue.

Although she tried not to, Barb began to worry as soon as the men dove below the surface. She told herself Walt had been in many tight spots, more in fact than most living men. She had even found herself in more than one dangerous spot and she had always come out OK. But, she knew from bitter firsthand experience, everyone didn't always come out OK. After a few minutes, she stood and started to pace the beach.

Out on the reef, Walt and Pierre swam along the outside edge. Walt scanned the bottom looking for anything that seemed out of place. A six-foot Whitetip Reef Shark prowled twenty feet away, out in the deeper water. Walt kept an eye on the shark, but he wasn't particularly worried. He knew the shark was only doing what sharks had done for millions of years. The shark was hunting, and smaller easier prey would be its target.

As Walt made his way along the edge of the reef, a Barracuda swam effortlessly past. Walt stopped and marveled at the torpedo like fish with its large eye and sharp, pointed teeth. Walt was ready to turn back when something caught his eye. A Parrotfish swam lazily along two feet above the reef, but it wasn't the Parrotfish that caught his eye. A large irregular object protruded from the coral. Motioning to Pierre, Walt kicked his fins and swam over to the object. Here, the surface of the sea was no more than five feet above the reef. The back and forth motion of the water made it difficult to stay still. Walt decided to dive deeper, down to the bottom, and he grabbed onto the edge of a rock formation. Pierre followed suit and hung onto the bottom next to Walt.

Walt lifted his head to get a better look at the object. The current pushed him away from the rock formation. The handhold gave way and Walt found himself holding a piece of coral encrusted rock. Only he didn't think it was rock at all. Walt drifted for a few feet before kicking his way back to a place beside Pierre. He grabbed a handhold again. Using his other hand, he stuffed the object into a mesh bag fastened to his belt.

Walt pointed at his eyes then to the object protruding from the coral reef signaling he was going to swim over and take a look. When Pierre nodded, Walt released his grip and swam hard. He stopped kicking as he reached the object. The current pushed him over and past the object and out to sea. Another wave came in and pushed Walt back over the object again. He used the momentum to swim close enough to Pierre to give him the signal to swim back to shore.

As soon as they got back on the island side of the reef, the water calmed. Walt surfaced and waited for Pierre. When his head broke the surface, Pierre removed his mouthpiece and asked, "Why did you come up? We could have seen what it was if we would have stayed down a little longer."

"I think I know what it is. Let's get in to the beach."

Waddling out of the ocean wearing flippers made the men look like oversized penguins. Barb wore a smile as she stood at the water's edge waiting for them.

"That was quick," she said.

Walt pulled his dive mask off. "It's a boat," he declared. "Looks like it's been down there for a while."

"What do you think happened?" Barb asked.

"The bow is broken up. I'd say it hit the reef and sank."

Pierre had been listening intently. He added, "Very common thing. Many times, it's younger men . . . maybe teenagers. They do not know the reefs like the older, more experienced men. Plus, they take bad chances."

"Like all teenagers," Barb said.

They walked up on the beach to where Barb's chair and the rest of the gear sat. Stripping out of the fins and dive gear, Walt showed Barb and Pierre the relic he'd brought back. When he scraped the crusted sea life away, he revealed fiberglass.

"Oh, yes," Pierre said. "That is from a local boat. Many men make their own boats here. The boats are built and fiberglassed by hand."

Walt nodded. "Yes, I thought it looked like homemade fiberglass."

They had arranged a pickup time for the helicopter, or they could call, and the pilot would come back earlier. Since the day was bright and sunny, they decided to wait for the helicopter to come back later that afternoon.

Walt didn't have much interest in the boat now that he knew what it was. Snorkeling would provide the entertainment for the remainder of the day. Walt and Barb donned snorkeling gear. Pierre stayed on land. He planned to find driftwood for a fire. They could roast a fish later if Walt speared one.

5

Staying inside the reef, they spent the next two hours exploring the tranquil water surrounding the island. Through his dive goggles, Walt could see the look of utter enjoyment on Barb's face as they explored the coral reef. Living plant systems grew on the reef and over thousands of years the reef grew in size. Stunning colors of red, white, and many shades of green carpeted the reef.

Time melted away. As the pair slowly finned through the crystal clear water, they saw Angelfish, Damselfish, and Butterflyfish. Walt and Barb swam close to schools of tiny baitfish and saw large clams along the inside of the reef. A school of Triggerfish attracted several small Reef Sharks. Manta rays, Skates, and a variety of other sea life prospered around the reef. Their journey had taken them half way around the atoll. On the way back, Walt used the spear gun he'd rented to take a medium-sized Grouper for lunch. As they came out of the water and onto the sandy beach Walt looked for Pierre, but didn't see him. Walt and Barb glanced at each other, shrugged, and continued to where the gear lay on the beach.

What he saw next sent chills down the length of his spine. Walt understood right away what had happened. The trail in the sand described everything. One set of foot prints came out of the thick brush. A large dark-red pool of congealed blood soaked into the sand. A trail of blood led back into the brush, but it wasn't merely a trail. Walt saw drag marks. From the evidence left in the sand, he knew someone had come out of the brush, done something to Pierre, and dragged him back into the brush.

Walt looked at Barb. He could tell by her expression she had also figured out what happened.

"Oh my God," she said.

Walt wasted no time in reloading the Floridian spear gun. The band powered, wooden spear gun was designed to work best under water, but other than the knives they had strapped to their calves, it was the only weapon they had. Walt had previously used a spear gun as a weapon, and he knew if used correctly the tool could have deadly results.

"We need to call the chopper," Barb said, digging in her bag for her phone. She stared at Walt and declared, "The phones are gone." She wasn't panicked, but Barb felt very nervous.

Walt glanced at his watch. The dial showed 12:30. "The helicopter won't be back until four. That's three and a half hours from now. We have to figure something out."

Barb threw a short-sleeved shirt on and pulled a pair of shorts over her swim suit bottom. Walt wore a T-shirt and his swim trunks.

As he stared at the path made by the drag marks, Walt said, "We should go after whoever did this."

With widening eyes, Barb said, "You've got to be joking."

"What choice do we have? We're sitting ducks if we sit around on the beach and wait for help."

"But look how dense the forest is," Barb pleaded. "Whoever did this could be waiting for us anywhere. We wouldn't know where until it's too late."

Barb had a good point, however Walt would rather be on the offensive than sitting around hoping to survive. "We could get picked off here. We're right out in the open."

Barb surveyed the island. The beach offered almost no cover. They could go into the brush farther on down the beach, but for all they knew, someone could be watching them at this very minute.

Just then, something struck Walt's leg. The object did not strike with much force, but he felt an immediate burning sensation. Looking down, Walt saw an arrow sticking out of his upper thigh. The shaft looked as though it was fashioned from bamboo and real bird feathers made up the veins.

Walt didn't see where the arrow came from, but Barb did. While Walt stared in disbelief at the arrow protruding from his leg, Barb saw a man kneeling on one knee just inside the brush. As she watched, he nocked another arrow and raised a primitive wooden bow.

The man aimed and released the arrow. Barb moved without thinking. As the deadly projectile arched through the air, she took a step and tackled Walt. The force of Barb's attack and the weight of her body knocked the unsuspecting Walt down. He ended up on his side with Barb on top of him. The arrow sailed over top of them.

For a second, when the arrow struck, Walt found himself stunned. The action of Barb plowing him to the ground made him snap out of his stupor and spring to life. From his position, laying on his side in the sand, Walt saw the man nock another arrow. Walt reacted with pure instinct. While other men might better Walter Ulrich in various areas of life, few could match his wits when it came to the instinct for survival.

He picked up the spear gun with his right hand. He knew the distance would be at the far range of effectiveness, but he had to try something. An arrow flew by his head. Without hesitation, Walt aimed and pulled the trigger. The small spear flew true. Walt didn't see exactly where the spear hit, but he heard the man grunt and saw him drop the bow.

The man inside the brush stood and looked down at his torso. The spear from Walt's shot protruded out from his midsection. Walt couldn't tell for certain, but he didn't think it penetrated very deep. Pushing Barb to the side, he came to his feet.

For the first time, Walt got a look at the man. Dirty, ragged clothes barely covered his lanky frame. He had sun darkened skin. A bandanna covered the top of his head. Long, straggly, gray hair fell to his shoulders. Walt and the stranger locked eyes for a moment. Then, the man reached down for the bow. Walt moved with deliberate actions wasting no time. He sprinted directly for his attacker. The man started to straighten up just as Walt slammed into him. Walt led with his shoulder hoping to bowl the man over. But the stranger reacted and blocked Walt's shoulder with the bow.

Walt careened off to the side. His rush carried enough momentum to drive the man to the ground, but not enough to do any serious damage.

Walt sprung to his feet. He pounced just as the other man stood. Both men hit the sand and rolled. Walt took a shot to the jaw from the end of the bow which the man still held. He delivered several quick punches to the man's midsection. The last one hit the spear which was still protruding from his abdomen. The man roared in pain. He rolled away breaking off the fight. Walt came to his feet ready to defend himself. However, the other man had enough. He turned and fled. Walt followed right on his heels.

Barb had the spear gun reloaded. She saw Walt take off after the attacker, and she ran hard to catch up. Both men disappeared into the heavy brush. Although Barb ran as hard as she could, she didn't gain any ground. Suddenly, she broke into a clearing. On one side of the small clearing stood a shack. Barb saw Walt chasing the man at the other edge of the clearing.

It looked as though Walt would catch up to the fleeing man, but then he stumbled. Walt recovered and stayed on his feet, but Barb detected a problem. His movements slowed dramatically. His actions began to look sleepy. Within a few more feet, Walt stumbled again. This time he went down and stayed down.

Barb ran to Walt's side. The atoll was not much more than a thin strip of land and from here, she could see the ocean on the opposite side of the island. Barb saw the man board what appeared to be a hand built outrigger canoe, and paddle hard out to sea. She turned her attention to Walt. His face was contorted in pain. He grasped his leg. The arrow remained lodged in his upper thigh muscle. Around the shaft of the arrow, the leg looked red and puffy.

"My leg is on fire," Walt groaned. "Hard to breathe."

"He must have dipped the tip in some type of poison." Barb looked at her surroundings. The canoe was out past the reef now. The man paddling pointed the bow toward one of the other tiny atolls which were scattered throughout the area.

"Think, Barb," she muttered under her breath. She knew

the island didn't offer any other way to get back to civilization. She focused her attention on the shack, then turned to Walt. "I'm going to see what's in that shack right over there. Will you be OK to wait here until I get back?"

He nodded, still in obvious pain.

Barb started for the shack. As she approached, she could see the man had tried to hide the dwelling by the way he had it camouflaged. Calling the crude structure a dwelling was a bit of a stretch. A glorified lean-to would have been a better description. The thatched roof was pitched toward the rear. Walls made of bamboo closed in three sides, leaving the front open.

Barb ducked inside and found what she was looking for right away. She returned to Walt. "Do you think you can walk over to that shack?" she asked.

"I'll try," Walt replied.

Barb helped him to stand. She slipped an arm around his shoulders to help support his weight. On shaky knees, he made his way over to the lean-to. Barb eased Walt to the bare ground inside the shelter. She gathered up some supplies from boxes and shelves along the walls.

"This might hurt, but we have to get the arrow out of your leg." Barb opened a half-full bottle of Scotch and poured a healthy dose on Walt's leg.

Walt grimaced, but stayed still.

Next Barb took a pair of pliers off the shelf. She tried to calm her shaking hands as she clamped the pliers onto the shaft of the arrow just above where it entered Walt's leg. She locked eyes with Walt. Without a word, Barb twisted the shaft and yanked back. With a pop and squirt of blood, the entire business end of the arrow pulled out.

This time, Walt gritted his teeth and groaned in pain.

Barb laid the arrow down and placed a clean bandage over the wound. "Keep pressure on that," she told Walt.

Small glass vials of liquid lined a shelf along one wall. Hand written labels adorned the vials. The names of marine animals were written on the labels. Over her shoulder, Barb asked, "Do you have any idea what the poison might be?"

"No. It could be anything."

"There's vials here. It looks like they could be serum or antivenom. The trouble is, I don't know which one to use."

"Tell me what they are."

Barb rattled off the unfamiliar names written on the vials.

Walt took a labored breath. He started to fade.

A wave of panic came over Barb. She had to do something. "Think, Barb," she told herself again. They had brought a first aid kit along. It should be back in the bag on the beach. "Walt, listen to me."

Walt opened his eyes and said, "I'm listening."

"I'm going to the beach for the first aid kit. I'll be right back."

"I understand," was all he could manage to say.

Barb placed her hand on his forehead. He had a fever, but she didn't think it was too high . . . yet. She patted his shoulder, stood, and headed out through the front opening. Barb pushed herself, running hard along the trail back to the beach. She picked up the bag and headed right back into the brush. Instead of following the same trail, she followed the blood trail, just in case Pierre was still alive.

Twenty yards inside the brush she found him. From a distance, Barb saw there was nothing she could do. Pierre's lifeless body lay face up in the weeds. Two arrows protruded from his chest and his throat had been cut. Barb walked up and stared down at the poor man. She felt a terrible sadness.

Pierre only came along to make a little money as a guide. He didn't deserve this. Barb did not linger long. She could not afford to spend time here while Walt was in trouble back at the lean-to. She turned to leave, but stopped when she noticed something out of the ordinary.

The ground where Pierre lay was a mixture of soil and sand. An arm's length away from the body there was a message scribbled in the ground. Pierre had used his last moments on earth to scrawl the words **Blue Ring Octopus** into the sand with his fingers. Barb stared for a long moment. That had to be it. Somehow, Pierre knew that the poison came from the deadly Blue Ring Octopus. Not wasting another moment, she doubled her effort and made it back to Walt in less than a minute.

Checking his fever, Barb faced the fact that Walt was fading fast. His ashen skin felt hot, and yet he shivered uncontrollably. Walt hovered on the edge of unconsciousness. Barb worried that if he slipped into a coma, he would never come out of it. Searching the containers on the shelf, Barb found what she was looking for.

Next, she fished around in the first aid kit until her hand closed on a hypodermic needle. Tearing the pack open, she removed the needle and plunger and drew a dose of liquid from a vial labeled Blue Ring Serum. Not knowing how much to use, Barb filled the syringe one quarter full. She assumed too little would be better than too much. Barb removed a rubber tourniquet from the kit and tied it tight around Walt's upper arm. When his vein became visible, she inhaled a deep breath, exhaled, and stuck the tip of the needle into Walt's arm.

Barb pushed the plunger and forced the liquid into Walt's blood stream. She could only hope that she was doing the right thing. If she did nothing, she felt certain he would die. However, if the serum was not the right antidote for the poison, or if she'd administered too much, she may have sealed Walt's fate. Loosening the tourniquet, Barb kissed Walt on the forehead and watched for a sign that she did the right thing. Walt showed no sign of change. After a few long minutes, Barb stood and went to the edge of the clearing. The canoe and the man who had attacked Walt were no longer visible.

In the three hours since receiving the serum, Walt's condition improved dramatically. By three-thirty in the afternoon, he was awake and coherent, although not yet ready to stand. Barb stayed by his side most of the time, giving him sips of water as he perked up. She also rummaged around the shelter. Among various unimportant items, she found a map and a description of an island.

6

A t four o'clock Barb walked to the beach to wait for the helicopter. As soon as she stepped out onto the sandy beach, she saw the small, streamlined helicopter coming in low. When it pulled up and hovered over the beach, Barb felt a deep sense of relief. The pilot set the helicopter down and killed the engine. When the rotor stopped spinning, Barb rushed toward the cockpit. She stopped short when she saw a second man sitting in the copilot's seat. The man had long hair and a scroll and spear tattoo on his neck.

She couldn't put her finger on it, but something just didn't sit right. A sense of foreboding came over her. The man in the copilot's seat got out and came around the front of the helicopter. As he neared, Barb started backpedaling. When he came into full view she saw the gun in his hand. Barb spun and ran without hesitation.

A bullet snapped past her head. Barb ran all out for the brush. She reached the edge when a slug flew through her right thigh just above her knee. Barb never stopped. She felt a burning sensation and warm blood running down her leg, but the shot did little to slow her down. In the safety of the brush, Barb ran along the trail, but soon came to a stop. She didn't want to lead the men back to the shack where Walt lay helpless. Finding a spot on the far side of a slight bend, she ducked into the thick brush and waited.

Soon, she heard footsteps. Barb knew the men were following her, but she wasn't sure of what she should do. She had the element of surprise on her side, but if the two men came along the trail at the same time, she didn't know how she could overpower both men without getting shot. The footfalls grew closer. Barb saw both the pilot and the copilot come around the bend. Without another thought for her safety, Barb popped up from her hiding spot and jumped on the second man.

The copilot led the way with the pilot following. Barb sprang on the pilot and clawed, grabbed, kicked, and punched. She caught the man by surprise and knocked him down. The gun he had been carrying flew from his hand. Barb fell on the gun, rolled, and pulled the trigger. Her shot flew high, but she continued shooting. The pilot accepted the fact that his gun had been taken. He did not attempt to get it back, but the man ducked his head, and ran back in the direction of the beach and waiting helicopter. Barb thought she clipped him with her last shot, but she wasn't sure.

Remembering the other man, Barb swiveled her hips and brought the gun around. She expected to feel a bullet tear into her at any second, but what she saw was totally unexpected. The man lay twitching on the trail beside where Barb lay. A spear from the spear gun stuck into his head at the base of his neck. Walt stood in the trail with the spear gun in his hand. His face looked pallid and he swayed slightly, but didn't fall.

Barb got to her feet as Walt stepped toward her. They embraced, and Barb asked, "How are you feeling?"

"Like I have the worst hangover a person could ever have."

"You saved my life," Barb said, her voice cracking with emotion.

"After you saved mine."

They heard the helicopter engine coming to life. Walt said, "Come on, maybe we can stop him from leaving."

When Barb tried to follow Walt, she stumbled and limped after him. Walt noticed the blood running freely down her leg. "What happened?"

Barb had forgotten the bullet wound until now. She looked at her leg and said, "I guess a bullet caught me." She also swayed on her feet slightly.

Walt didn't think the bullet hit bone or she wouldn't be able to stand and talk about it the way she did. However, he didn't feel comfortable with the amount of blood she was losing. "Sit down, I'll have a look."

"What about the chopper? We have to stop him."

"Sit," Walt said, insisting.

Barb sat and when Walt removed his shirt and wiped the blood away, he saw a neat hole in her thigh. Checking the front of her thigh, he saw the exit wound. The slug had gone straight through the muscle, but Walt felt certain it had not hit bone. His greatest concern was the loss of blood. He applied pressure to the wound by holding his shirt against the bullet hole.

Walt didn't want to stay on the trail for long. When the bleeding slowed to a trickle, he wrapped Barb's leg with the T-shirt and helped her to her feet. As Walt was finishing up, he heard the sound of the helicopter as it lifted into the air and banked away. Soon the noise faded, and they were alone again on the tiny coral atoll.

Walt took a second to pick up the gun the copilot had dropped. He stuffed it, along with the gun Barb had, into his waistband. Together, the two beleaguered day-trippers limped and staggered their way back to the shelter.

When they got inside, Walt had Barb lay in the same spot where Walt had lain earlier. Walt used the first aid kit to clean and bandage Barb's leg.

He gave her a small shot of whiskey and chided, "Wait until Brock hears you got shot again. You'll never hear the end of it."

Barb threw back the drink. Walt's comment caused her to cough. "I know. I can't believe I got shot more times than he did."

Walt kissed her full on the lips feeling the burn of the scotch. When he broke away, he said, "We need to figure out how to get off this island."

"Do you think anyone will search for us?"

"I don't know. The problem is, we have no idea who that nut shooting arrows was, or how the helicopter guys are connected to him."

"There's a map over there," Barb pointed to the shelf along the wall. "Maybe there's something that can help."

Walt unfolded the map. The atoll they were currently strandedon was clearly marked. Several smaller atolls were also shown. The biggest had markings, but Walt couldn't work out their meaning. He asked Barb, "Which island was he paddling toward?"

Barb examined the map and pointed to the largest island, the one with the markings. "This is definitely the one."

Walt thought things over for a moment. He spoke with

definite determination in his voice. "We'll have to pay this character a visit. We can make a raft out of something, I don't know what yet, but he won't expect us. We should be able to take him by surprise."

"What about the pilot?"

"If anyone comes back, I want us to be as far from here as we can get."

Barb nodded. She looked tired. Walt figured she was weak from the loss of blood. His thoughts went to the weapons they had. "One other thing we have going for us is the gun you took from the pilot. If he's armed with a primitive bow and we have two guns, he made a big mistake in picking a fight with us."

Walt elevated Barb's leg and ordered her to get some rest. She sleepily agreed. Although he didn't feel one hundred percent, he felt his strength quickly returning. Walt wasted no time scouring the area for material to use for a raft. He found a few wide boards and a coil of rope right behind the shack. With his dive knife, he cut lengths of rope and bamboo. Over the next two hours, Walt fashioned a crude raft out of the materials at hand.

With the sun low on the horizon, Walt returned to the shack. He wanted to have the raft finished as soon as possible and focused on that task. Now that the work was done, he had to make up his mind as to what to do next. On one hand, he wanted to go right away. The problem was, by the time he got Barb onto the raft and set out for the distant island, it would be dark. Making the trip in broad daylight would be risky. Attempting it at night could be disastrous. If the raft flipped or sank, he'd have a tough time keeping Barb with him while he swam to land. In another scenario, they could float right past the tiny atoll. Who knew where the currents would take them. Walt didn't have the materials or tools to construct a more durable raft. A short trip would be about all the hastily made raft could handle.

On the other hand, if the pilot came back with gun-toting friends, he didn't want to be caught flat-footed. After mulling the situation over, he finally came up with a compromise. They would stay in the shack. Barb could use the rest and so could he. In the case of the helicopter return-ing, he would wake Barb and hurry to the raft to hopefully float away undetected.

Before the light had completely faded, Walt went to where he'd shot the copilot on the trail. He retrieved the spear from the back of the man's head. It was the only one he had left. The spear gun had saved their lives twice already that day, and he thought the weapon could come in handy in the future.

When he returned, he found Barb sleeping. She breathed lightly which Walt took as a good sign. As the darkness settled in around the shelter, Walt listened to the sounds of the untamed paradise and wondered how the first Europeans felt when they had discovered these isolated islands centuries ago. He needed rest, but resolved to stay awake. Barb's life, along with his own, depended on it.

7

An hour before daylight, Walt woke Barb. He couldn't believe she smiled as she roused from the deep sleep she'd been in. He'd kept a close eye on her throughout the night, and judging by her snoring, Walt didn't think a person could have slept more soundly.

"Good morning," he said. "How are you feeling?"

Barb had not come fully awake yet and wasn't sure how she felt. She stretched and felt the pain in her leg. "My leg is sore."

Walt nodded. His own leg caused him a good deal of pain. The serum Barb had injected him with did wonders counteracting the poison in his system. However, the actual wound worried Walt. Infection was a concern and the red swollen tissue around the entry hole didn't look good.

He gave her a sip of water from a bottle they had along in their bag.

Barb drank and asked, "Has anything changed?"

Walt shook his head, "No. The helicopter hasn't been back and no one else has come to this island. However, we need to get started right away just to ensure we stay one step ahead of whoever is coming back." He brushed a length of hair from her face. "Are you able to stand?"

"I'll try." Leaning heavily on Walt, Barb brought herself to her feet. She could put weight on her bad leg, but the more weight she placed on it, the more pain she felt.

Walt took it as a good sign. At least she could stand and move, even if a little slowly. "I'll help you down to the raft, then come back and load all our supplies. Once we're loaded it should be light enough to make the trip."

Walt spent the next forty minutes preparing the raft. As he predicted, dawn had broken over the South Pacific when he was finished.

Barb had a worried look on her face all morning. Walt put his arm around her shoulders and looked toward the pink sky in the east. "Isn't it beautiful?"

Barb smiled. "Yes, it is," she replied. "I just hope we can get out of this mess. Our friends know we went to Tahiti, but it is very possible no one knows we're here on this exact island. Unlike our last hazardous adventure in Morocco, we have none of our own people coming to help us. By the time someone realizes we're missing, it could be too late."

"That's why we have to take control of the situation. We can't sit around playing defense and waiting for help."

"I know. It feels a bit lonely is all, just you and me."

"It's you and me against the world, babe," Walt said in his best Humphrey Bogart impression.

Speaking in his natural voice, Walt added, "Besides, they're all hazardous adventures. We're not alone. We have each other and we'll just have to figure a way out of this ordeal."

Barb smiled. Together, they boarded the hastily slapped together raft and got ready for their voyage.

Neither Walt nor Barb could possibly know, but they

weren't alone. One of their own was on the way, and he was exactly the one man they'd pick if they wanted someone to come and help.

———

Brock McGowen didn't have anything on his schedule for the next week or two. His girlfriend's new job kept her very busy. She started working for Kendall Outdoors and she needed to focus her full attention on learning and adapting to her new position with the company. Being Barb Kendall's personal assistant entailed a broad range of duties, and Martha would require some time to adapt. Brock thought this would be perfect timing to get away for a week or so. He couldn't think of a better way to spend a week than with his oldest and closest friend, Walter Ulrich.

The two had been friends for years. Before striking it rich on a treasure hunt, they worked together as Federal Mining Engineers. Although both men were financially secure and neither man had to work, both Brock and Walt worked for the Seven Seas Television Channel. Brock worked as a sub-contractor taking on whatever situation Walt handed him. Walt produced the show and when he needed some type of specialized work done, he often called Brock. Both men were extremely satisfied in their roles with the company.

Brock spent the night at the Blue Pearl Hotel on the island of Tahiti. The twelve-hour flight from Minneapolis to Papeete, along with the many drinks he'd consumed aboard the plane, drained his energy, and made him drowsy. Walt hadn't mentioned which hotel he was staying at when he left the message on Brock's voice mail, only that he was staying in Tahiti.

Brock checked the desk when he arrived and found that Walt was not staying at that hotel. No matter, Brock knew he'd find him at one of the others. Tahiti wasn't a very large island and Brock had good detective skills. He checked into his room, showered, and turned in for the night.

When the first rays of sunlight hit the roof of the hotel, Brock was already up and out the door. He wanted to find his friend while it was still early, in case he had something planned. The stocky Midwesterner took a cab to every one of the resorts in the cove. At each hotel, Brock went to the desk and inquired about Walt. Finally, he found the right one, but when the desk clerk called the room, there was no answer.

Brock had a jovial, outgoing personality. He had a way of getting people to open up and talk, sometimes more than they should. When the clerk told him a Mrs. Kendall was also staying in Walt's room, Brock raised an eyebrow. "No wonder he's not answering," he mused, smiling.

With everything loaded on the raft, Walt pushed off. As he got into deeper water, he picked up speed. He was running through the crystal clear water when he jumped onto the raft beside Barb. Walt clambered to a sitting position and the two sat side by side. He had fashioned paddles from old planks of lumber he found lying around behind the shack. As they began to paddle, the raft made headway, but didn't exactly skim over the waves. The contraption plowed through the water with its platform flush or slightly under water.

Once they got past the rougher water over the reef, the raft handled fine. By this time Walt and Barb had picked up on how to control the bulky craft. Paddling also needed moving their hips to maintain balance as much as stroking the water with the paddles. Walt marveled at the clarity of the water while they paddled along. He could see clear to the shallow bottom during the whole trip. This remote Archipelago was truly an unspoiled area of the planet. He ventured a sideways glance at Barb. His emotions threatened to overwhelm him as he watched her paddle. Although both Barb and he had been wounded and would surely be hunted down, Walt relished the idea of working for Seven Seas. He felt lucky to be able to travel to such remote places and live an adventurous life. On this trip, he even had the woman he loved by his side.

A slight current wanted to push the raft to the northwest of the atoll. Walt and Barb had to adjust their paddling to point the bow toward the south-eastern tip. The current seemed stronger as they neared land and the raft sank lower as they fought the current.

Finally, Walt said, "That's it. We should be able to make it from here. Let's paddle straight ahead and go with the current."

Barb complied and the two of them paddled with easy strokes. The reef wasn't as prominent around this atoll; therefore, the last leg of the voyage went smoothly. They directed the raft to a tiny sand beach in a protected cove. When they were still fifty yards from shore, Walt heard the familiar thumping of rotors. Without seeing the aircraft, he knew a helicopter was approaching.

Walt turned to see Barb staring over her shoulder. As they watched, a tiny black dot became larger and at last, a helicopter materialized. They continued paddling and hoped the pilot wouldn't spot them. The helicopter hovered over the atoll they had come from, then dropped to the beach and out of sight.

At last, the water was shallow enough for Walt to jump out of the raft. He waded to shore, towing the raft with one hand. When he beached the bulky raft, Walt noticed a disturbance in the sand. He assisted Barb onto the beach before unloading their gear.

Handing one of the guns to Barb, he said in a low voice, "He's here."

Barb took the handgun and stuck it in her waistband. "How do you know?"

Walt pointed to the sandy beach. The strip of beach was no more than ten or twelve yards wide from the water's edge to the trees. "Look," Walt said, pointing. "See how the sand is disturbed there. He used something . . . a bush or something, and brushed away his footprints. It's pretty obvious."

"Yes, I see it, but where's his boat?"

"Good question," Walt said, glancing around. "Let's get our raft up into the brush. At least it will be out of sight in case our friends in the helicopter come looking for us."

"With friends like those, who needs enemies?" Barb asked as she lent a hand.

With a great amount of effort, the pair dragged the raft up the beach and into the brush. Walt used broken branches to hide the raft. He too, brushed the footprints in the sand away. "Doesn't hurt to be careful," he said.

A faint trail led inland from the beach. With Walt leading the way, they followed the trail with their guns at the ready. Although it made walking more difficult, they carried all the equipment on their backs including the scuba gear. With everything that had happened, Walt wanted to be certain they wouldn't be caught without something they needed. After only a short distance, they came across a trickle of a stream. Walt knelt and tasted the water. "Fresh water, that's hard to believe on such a small piece of land. "Walt and Barb hiked another forty yards and saw the reason for the fresh water.

A rocky outcrop broke up the dense jungle. Trees and plants sprouted up from crevices in the rocks and the whole outcrop rose about six feet from the ground. In the center of the craggy rocks, a stream flowed from an underground spring.

Barb said, "All the rain water on the atoll must flow into this drainage."

Walt shook his head in wonder. "Yeah, it's amazing." He knelt and drank cool water from his cupped hands. He smiled at Barb. "Try some. It's probably as clean as any water we've ever drank."

Barb needed help to kneel. When Walt helped her down, she drank thirstily from the spring. Barb finished drinking and started to stand. Something in the rocks caught her eye. Walt reached down to help, but she stopped him. "Wait. I think I see something."

Walt's eyes followed her gaze. He merely saw the rocky outcropping and the spring.

"It's in between that crack," Barb said. When she raised her head, she lost sight of it, but when she ducked her head, she saw it again. "Help me over there."

Walt gave her a helping hand and stepped arm in arm with her right up to the wet rocks. Barb bent over at the waist and peered at a crack just to the side of the flowing water. She grabbed hold of a tree root that stuck out of a crevice and pulled down. Barb wanted to break the root off to get it out of the way, so she could see better, but the root didn't break. When it moved, the root worked as a lever. It lowered slowly and as it did, a large shelf of rock slid back along one side of the crevice creating an opening.

Barb took a stunned step back as she watched the shelf slide.

Walt moved in closer. He heard the grating sound of stone rubbing against stone and felt the ground shaking slightly. Looking into the opening, he could see some sort of chamber. The damp smell of earth escaped the opening.

"What the hell is this?" Barb asked.

"Let's find out." Walt used the dive light to illuminate the dark passage as they stepped seemingly right into the earth.

8

The light revealed a small room about ten-feet square. The floor consisted of dirt while the ceiling and walls were solid rock. On one side of the room, Walt saw a passageway leading farther into the earth. A table made of lashed together bamboo stood in the middle of the room. Other than the table, the room was empty. Walt led Barb to the table. A thick tablet lay on the table. Barb opened it and started to read.

This is the story of Oligand, recorded by Ricardo Baez. The Oligand was a vast treasure deposited on an atoll by Spanish explorers in the year 1705. According to the ship's log, the treasure was taken from the western coast of South America, probably from Chile. That is where I first heard of the fantastic story from some locals while I was on an expedition to find a lost Mayan City.

Oligand was the name of the Spanish ship carrying the treasure. Instead of returning to Spain to deliver the fortune to the Monarchy, the Captain and crew decided to keep the treasure and live the high life in the islands of the South Pacific. Somehow, probably from the sailors bragging, the Chieftains and Nobles knew the gold had been stolen, first from the indigenous people of Chile, then from Spain. The islanders acted swiftly, and the Captain and crew were killed by the Tauri tribe who hoarded the treasure and guarded its whereabouts. This tribe is extremely secretive and remained undiscovered until 1997 when I happened upon them.

I have cataloged the treasure. You will find the records of the entire treasure within these pages.

Be warned. A supernatural High Priest guards over the treasure. The Tauri people believe that if the ill-gotten treasure is removed or lost, the Gods will punish their entire tribe. Therefore, they protect it with their lives. The local people also believe this island is haunted. They call the treasure Tapu, which translates into Taboo, and that is the reason they do not come after me. Over the years I have spent alone here on this island, I have come to believe the legend. The treasure is Taboo, and I will never present this find to the public out of fear and respect for human life. I assume I will be long dead by the time anyone reads this. I only ask that I be remembered as the world's greatest discoverer.

Ricardo Baez

Walt and Barb took a glance at each other.

After a brief pause, Walt said, "That explains the crazy guy on the beach shooting arrows at us."

"Yes, that explains a lot. According to this, he's been here since 1997."

"No wonder he's lost his mind," Walt mused. "These islands are beautiful but extremely remote. Humans need interaction with other humans to stay sane."

Barb nodded in agreement. "This might also explain why the helicopter pilot and copilot wanted to do us harm. They did both have the same tattoo on their neck." She hesitated, then asked, "Could they be from a long-lost tribe?"

"At this point I wouldn't discount anything."

"This is truly amazing. If what this says is real . . . can you imagine the series of events that led to this tablet. I mean lost tribes, supernatural Priests, Spanish treasures, this is a fantastic story."

Walt chuckled. "I don't know what it all means, but I am glad to finally have an idea of what's going on here. When people are trying to kill you and you have no idea why, it's a bad situation."

"I agree. I feel as though a weight has been lifted off my shoulders."

Walt gestured toward the passageway leading off the main chamber. "Want to find out what else is in here?"

"After you, darling," Barb said with a smile.

Walt led the way through a narrow passage. They had to crouch down to avoid scraping their heads on the low, rock ceiling. The passageway opened out into another room. This room appeared to be about the same size as the first one although the vast amount of treasure piled up to the ceiling made it hard to determine the room's actual size.

The glint of gold almost blinded Walt as he shone the flashlight into the room. Thousands of pieces of gold were heaped up covering almost the entire space. A narrow path led to the middle of the room, but everything else was covered with gold. Walt saw no silver, no pewter or bronze, only gold.

"My God!" Barb exclaimed. "Can you believe it?"

"If I wasn't standing here staring at it, I don't think I could."

They stared wide-eyed at hundreds of crudely molded gold bars. Thousands of gold coins lay in deep piles on the floor. Stacks of gold necklaces, bracelets, and rings were mixed in among the rest of the gold. The room contained enormous wealth.

"This treasure is worth millions upon millions, not to mention the historical value. I can't comprehend how it can be squirreled away like this for all these years," Barb said.

"I know what you mean. Right now, I think we need to figure out a way to get back to civilization. Let's go outside and discuss our options."

With Walt leading the way, they went back into the other room. Before they could get to the narrow opening, a loud bang shuddered through the cave. Walt and Barb instinctively ducked as the ground shook and dust fell from the ceiling. The light from outside was cut off as heavy rocks came down and blocked off the entrance.

The rocks also cut off their escape route. When the dust settled, Barb coughed. "What happened?"

Walt said, "That was no accident. Someone really doesn't want this treasure to be discovered." He hurried to the blocked entrance and listened. He hoped to hear someone speaking. He thought maybe he could learn something about what had happened. Other than the ringing in his ears caused by the loud explosion, all he heard was silence.

Despite the tons of rock blocking the entrance, the air inside the chamber remained fresh. Walt didn't think that would last long. "We need to find a way out of here," he told Barb.

She looked around uncomfortably. "This looks pretty solid."

"You're talking to an old miner," he reminded her. "If there is any way out, I'll find it. Let's start by checking the other room."

Barb marveled at Walt's resolve. Nothing ever seemed to get to him. Though the situation seemed dire, she felt happy with her choice of a man.

One at a time they entered the room full of gold. Walt listened for a few seconds. He didn't see the stream of water like he could from the first chamber. However, he could hear running water. It sounded close, but muffled. He got on his knees and began to dig through the pile of gold coins.

"What is it, Walt?"

He dug harder. "I'm not sure, but I think there's something here."

Barb watched for a moment before joining in and helping him dig. Soon, her fingers were sore and bleeding from digging through the hard, rough edged gold coins. As they got closer to the stone floor, they noticed the coins were wet.

Walt reached the floor and announced, "It's here." He looked at Barb. "There's an underground stream here."

The enormous fortune of gold proved to be a burden and the couple found it difficult to clear the floor. Walt dug down to the stone floor while Barb threw the handfuls of gold into the passage just to get it out of the way. Soon they had a large area of floor cleared. In one spot, there was a hole about two and a half feet across. The hole was filled with seawater. Walt didn't know how deep the water was, but when he stuck his hand in it, he didn't touch bottom.

Barb focused on the hole and concentrated. "What is that?"

Walt took a deep breath. "It's an underground stream. It could be a way out or it could be a dead end, it's hard to say." After a pause to think about it, he added, "The atoll is very small. The chances of this stream going on for a great distance aren't too great."

"But it could tighten up. The stream could narrow down to a trickle."

Walt took a second to decide. He looked her in the eye.

"We have to try it, Barb. There's no other way out and whoever used explosives to seal the entrance could also bring this whole place down on top of us."

"OK, but I have to tell you. I'm extremely nervous about this."

"You have to trust me. We'll swim along this stream until we come out together."

Barb nodded in agreement.

Walt started to get the air tanks ready. They had plenty of air left, so he did not think that would be a problem. He placed both handguns and a few other items in the mesh diving bag and fastened it to the waistband of his shorts with a short piece of rope. He strapped the dive knife to his calf. Barb did the same.

Barb had never used self-contained underwater breathing apparatus — scuba gear, before. Normally, she would have gotten some formal training from a certified diver, but the dire situation would not allow such a luxury. Also, under normal circumstances both divers would have a dive master monitoring the dive from above. Due to the limited time frame they had to work with, Walt merely ran through the basics. With Barb's intelligence, he figured she could absorb most of what he told her. The last instruction he gave was a run through of the universal hand signals. Barb memorized them on the second time through.

When they were ready, Walt gave Barb a friendly pat on the shoulder and smiled at her. Her breath came fast. She found it hard to take a full, deep breath. The truth was, she had never been so scared in her life.

Walt understood her concern. The underground stream looked tight. If it did peter out, he didn't think there would be enough room to get turned around and go back. Also, with the tight spaces came a chance of equipment getting snagged or damaged. In reality, Walt knew they would need a healthy dose of luck.

With the preparations done and the speculation going nowhere good, the time had come. Walt slipped into the small hole in the floor. Cool water swirled around his body and legs. He thought that was a good sign. The fact that the water was moving meant it had to be going somewhere.

Barb came in next. The confined space left little room for movement. Walt did not dawdle. He didn't want to end up one or two minutes short of air. With a nod to Barb, he dove under the surface. The clarity of the water surprised even Walt. However, as soon as he got away from the dim filtered light of the cave, unbroken darkness closed in around him. He reached up and adjusted the dive light he wore on his head. With his dive light adjusted he could see the stream bottom. Looking ahead, he could see the narrow stream heading into darkness. Walt moved ahead and waited for Barb. When he saw her feet sink down through the water from above he started moving forward into the tunnel. He kicked slowly with his arms out in front of him, allowing the slight current to help carry him along.

As he finned along for the first thirty yards, the width of the stream stayed about the same. Although the sides did not close in, tree roots wound into the tube-like tunnel. The roots began to scrape and cling to his air tank and air hoses. Walt slowed his progress. Now moving ahead at a snail's pace, he had more time to push the obstructive roots out of the way.

9

Fifty yards from where they started, the passage suddenly narrowed. The current picked up and before Walt could react, he was sucked into the narrower tunnel. Walt reached out and grabbed onto some roots to slow his progress however, he could not maintain a decent hold. Water rushed by his head as the current picked up even more speed. The next thing he knew, Walt felt himself flying through the tunnel like a kid zooming down a tube on a water slide.

He felt the sides constrict and squeeze against his side. If the tunnel closed another few inches, he'd be stuck. Then, he came free. The current pushed Walt into a larger chamber. Walt tumbled head over heels through the clear water. He righted himself just in time to see Barb somersaulting into the bigger chamber.

He reached out and grabbed her arm, steadying her in the process. In the clear water, he noticed Barb's eyes were wide, but she soon calmed down. Walt winked at her and she smiled. He surveyed the cavernous chamber, then motioned for Barb to follow. With Barb at his side, he kicked his fins and headed for what he thought was up. In the darkness, Walt found it hard to determine direction. He was surprised to find himself breaking the surface of the water. Barb surfaced to his side. Walt took off his goggles, spat out his mouthpiece and inhaled a breath. The air tasted slightly stale, but it contained plenty of oxygen.

Barb followed suit and asked, "Where are we?"

"I don't know. This is a massive chamber." He glanced around as he treaded water. Only feet separated his face from the solid rock ceiling and walls. "I think it's an ancient volcanic streambed. We'll have to find out where the water is draining from this chamber. We'll go back down and look around. How are you doing?"

Barb flashed a brave smile. "I didn't care for that tight spot, but I'm hanging in there."

"You're doing great. Like I said, this atoll isn't very big; we have to be close to the open ocean." Walt took a few deep breaths and winked at Barb. "Ready?"

Barb nodded and replaced her goggles and mouthpiece.

When Walt was ready, he gave the signal to dive, then headed down. The pristine water provided very good visibility. When they got down to where they could feel the current again, Walt turned in the opposite direction. In a short distance, he found the far wall. The current seemed to drop below the diver's feet. With Barb at his heels, Walt dove deeper. Right at the bottom, where the walls met the floor, there was a short crack. Walt could see a rectangular opening right at the bottom of the chamber.

When Walt got down and looked through the opening, he thought he could see a difference in colors. He stared another moment, then gave Barb the thumbs-up signal to surface.

When they broke the surface, and removed their goggles

and mouthpieces, Walt said, "I think that opening right along the streambed is where the water's going out to sea."

Between heavy breathing Barb asked, "What makes you think that?"

"When I looked out I could see colored water. It looks to be more of a brighter, green color. I'm certain it's because the stream is meeting the sea. I'm not a geologist, but I'd be willing to bet lava once flowed through there creating the tunnel."

"That opening is pretty tight," Barb said. "Do you think we can get through it?"

Walt shook his head. "Not while we're wearing our air tanks."

"You're suggesting we take off our tanks?"

"Yes, exactly. We'll hold our breath, swim through and come out in the sea."

From the way she stared at him, Walt knew she was mulling the idea over in her head. In a reassuring tone, he said, "It's the only thing I can think of. We'll dive to the bottom, fill our lungs with air, take off our tanks, and swim out to sea."

Barb opened her mouth to say something, but Walt cut her off. "If we can't get out to sea, we'll swim back against the current. It isn't that strong down there."

"OK, Walt," Barb said quietly. "I'm with you."

He touched her face. "Just think of the stories we can tell when we're old."

Barb forced a smile. "No one will believe us."

Walt grinned. "You're probably right." He almost felt overcome with emotion. Barb was not the type of woman who panicked or fretted about things she could not change. She put her trust in his decision. In a serious tone, he asked, "You ready?"

"I'm ready, let's go."

They replaced their gear and kicked for the bottom. Settling on the hard rock floor, they inhaled deep breathes. Walt looked at Barb and nodded. She inhaled deeply and began to remove her air tank. Walt did the same thing. He gestured for Barb to follow as he ducked under the rocky ceiling. Walt used steady breast strokes at the entrance to the narrow tunnel. Barb was a reasonable swimmer and very athletic, but she could not match his swimming ability. He knew Barb was behind him, but he didn't want to get too far ahead. As he got farther in, he could see the color of the water was turning a darker shade of green. Walt knew the open ocean was not far away. He also knew the space was closing in. The ceiling sloped downward, pinching the opening tighter and tighter. Walt could feel the saltwater against his skin. He saw the end of the rock formation a short twenty yards away. Walt kept his arms outstretched in front of him and used his fins to propel his body forward. He gave a powerful kick but found himself coming to a stop. He struggled but the action only made the situation worse. He couldn't move forward or back. Suddenly, he felt Barb slam into his legs. Her momentum forced him forward and into a wider space. Walt struggled and fought his way free at last. He felt the mesh bag tear away from his belt, but never gave it a second thought. With lives at stake, there was no time to worry about the bag.

Barb's body was about as thick as Walt's and he knew Barb would not get through. He braced his arms against the rocky roof stopping his movement. Walt waited to feel Barb coming behind him. Nothing happened. With every ounce of his strength, he used his arms to push himself backward. Inch by inch, he moved back against the current. At last he felt a hand grasping at his leg. Walt shook his leg and hoped

Barb would get the hint. Several more times, he felt her hand brush his leg.

Walt's breath wouldn't hold out for long. The cardiovascular energy needed to push himself backward against the current and to hold himself there almost depleted his oxygen. He pushed harder and moved backward another six inches. At last, he felt Barb grab his ankle with both hands. Her grip felt firm. Walt hoped she could hold on tight enough. He'd only get one chance at this.

With one mighty push, Walt shoved off from the ceiling. He only moved an inch. Walt coiled his body as much as he could. Reaching up, he placed his hands on the rock ceiling and mustered every ounce of his strength. He pushed off with all the energy he could muster. This time, he moved ahead. To her credit, Barb held on to his ankle. Walt used his hands to push off the rock over and over, slowly making his way along the tunnel. After about ten feet, he got into more open space where the passage widened.

Walt now used his arms to swim. He stroked hard to move forward. The mouth of the stream opened into the vast expanse of the Pacific. Suddenly, they found themselves swimming in wide open water. A large Angelfish fish spooked when it saw the intruders.

Walt glanced at Barb. She had already started to swim for the surface. Walt could tell she was doing fine. The only obstacle now was getting to the surface fast enough. Luckily, they were only about fifteen feet below the surface. Walt stayed by Barb's side on their ascent. She swam hard and made good progress, until she slowed just five feet from the surface. Walt moved in without hesitation. He grabbed her arm and assisted her for the last few feet.

They both broke into the air at the same time. While

they tread water, Walt and Barb inhaled deep breaths of sweet air.

When she was able, Barb looked at Walt, laughed and wrapped her arms around him. Walt hugged her back, but soon had to pry her arms away. She held on so tight she almost sank him.

"We made it," Barb said. "We actually made it."

Walt laughed harder. "Let's get in to shore. We'll be safe there."

As they swam toward land, Walt saw the beach where they landed the raft. He gestured in that direction.

After a short swim, they staggered up the sandy beach. At the edge of the beach where the sand met the foliage, Walt and Barb collapsed. Their chests heaved as they breathed hard. Both Walt and Barb felt pain from their leg injuries but overall, they felt ecstatic just to be alive.

Walt sat up suddenly. Far in the distance, he saw something out on the ocean. It looked like little more than a speck until he placed his hand on his forehead to shade his eyes. He could make out a paddling motion. A man sat in an outrigger canoe. The man was paddling the canoe toward a distant, smaller atoll.

"What is it?" Barb asked, noticing Walt's interest.

"It looks like our friend is leaving. I can see him paddling his canoe for another island."

"He must think we're dead . . . or trapped underground for good," Barb said. "That's twice he tried to kill us. He must really want to keep the treasure secret."

"I wonder why? Most explorers crave the recognition brought on by discovering something lost. You'd think he would want to bask in the glory of finding such an enormous treasure."

"Who knows? If he's been out here since 1997, he could have all kinds of mental problems."

Walt agreed. As usual, Barb's assessment was spot on. "Yes, I'm with you. He must have some skeletons in his closet . . . staying out here all this time. At least we have an idea of what's going on now."

"That's right. Not knowing who was trying to kill us, or why, was the worst part . . . well, not the worst part. There were too many worst parts to mention now."

Barb sat up and shaded her eyes. As soon as she came to a sitting position, an arrow flew into the ground where she had been laying. Walt and Barb stared at the quivering handcrafted arrow for what seemed like a long moment. Then they scrambled, with Walt rolling to one side, Barb to the other.

Another arrow struck a tree and lodged in its trunk. If Walt hadn't rolled behind the tree, the arrow would have hit him. After how sick he'd become from the first arrow that had been impaled in his leg, he didn't want to get hit again. Walt sprinted ten yards along the beach to where the sand ended. He turned and ran into the brush hoping to outflank the attacker.

Barb found herself alone. She rolled to her side and came to a stop in a prone position. Staying completely still, she didn't think whoever had ambushed them could see her. Barb didn't expect Walt to go the other way. The move had taken her by surprise and now she feared for his life. For the second time in the past hour, Barb tried to control her breathing and not hyperventilate.

Walt watched his footing, but he didn't dwell on keeping perfectly silent. He wanted to get close and rush the man. Pulling the dive knife from the sheath strapped to his thigh, he steadily made his way toward where he thought the arrow came from.

A twig snapped ten feet in front of Walt. He froze for a second, then attacked. As he broke into a small clearing, Walt saw the same man with the bandanna and long gray hair. He was the same man Walt had shot with the spear gun. The man spun to face Walt. He tried to raise the bow, but reacted too late. Walt struck with the knife as he ran forward. The blade sunk deep into the man's chest. His fist connected with the man's jaw sending him sprawling backward.

Walt was not a killer. He merely wanted to survive. Before the man could resume his attack, Walt pounced on him. "Ricardo!" he shouted. "Stop. Ricardo, we don't want to steal the treasure."

Understanding registered in the man's eyes. A slight smile formed on his face.

Walt thought he might be able to talk with the explorer, but it was too late. Ricardo Baez groaned. When Walt examined him, he noticed the wound in his chest looked bad. Worse than that however, was the arrow sticking through his ribs. When he fell, he somehow landed on one of his own poisoned arrows. The entire shaft went into his back and out through his abdomen.

Walt kicked the bow away and knelt beside the mortally wounded man. Ricardo Baez started speaking, but his words were cut short when he started coughing up blood. Walt knew he wouldn't last long.

The time for getting to know the man had passed. He didn't have long to live, and Walt wasn't about to try to deceive him. He got right to the point. "Why are you trying to kill us?"

Ricardo answered in a weak voice, "You cannot take the

treasure. It is guarded and Tapu." He coughed some more. When he spoke again, his voice sounded distant. "The Tauri tribe will perish if the treasure is lost . . ."

Walt saw the life drain from Ricardo Baez. He ran his fingers softly over the man's eyes closing them forever. When Ricardo had passed, Walt pulled his knife from Ricardo's chest, not because he didn't want anyone to know he'd killed the man, but he thought he might need it again. After looking around, he went back to the beach and found Barb.

When she saw Walt walking toward her, Barb stood and asked, "What happened?"

"It was Ricardo. He tried to kill us to prevent us from taking the treasure."

"Is he . . ."

Walt nodded. "He's dead."

Barb studied Walt for a moment. "Are you all right?"

"Yes. You were right, he was too far gone. He said the Tauri tribe would perish if the treasure was taken. Did you ever hear of the Tauri tribe?"

"No, but there's probably a lot of tribes I don't know about. Did he say anything else?"

Walt shook his head. "That's all."

Barb thought for a second as she looked out to sea. "If Ricardo's dead, who is that?"

Walt followed her gaze to the man paddling the canoe far in the distance. He looked like little more than a speck now. "I don't know. Maybe it's an evil spirit."

"Whoever it is was definitely on this island."

Barb's last words were almost drowned out by the sound of the helicopter taking off. As they watched, the helicopter rose above the tree tops of the nearby island, hovered for a second, then began to fly toward their position. Walt could see it was the same Enstrom Turbine 480B they'd flown in the previous day. "Let's get out of the open," he said.

They ran to where Ricardo lay. Walt dragged the lifeless body into the underbrush and used branches as cover. As the noise from the helicopter's blades grew louder, Walt and Barb ducked under some heavy brush. The tactic failed.

Someone aboard the helicopter must have noticed movement. The craft circled first, then hovered above where they were positioned. Above the roar of the whirling blades, Walt heard the unmistakable crack of a rifle shot. A slug slammed into the ground three feet from where they hid under some bushes.

"We have to move!" Walt yelled, grabbing Barb by the hand. He pulled her to her feet and they both took off running for the far side of the island. Walt heard the report of another rifle shot. The occupants of the helicopter wanted them dead. He believed it would be useless to surrender.

With Barb right on his heels, Walt passed the entrance to the cave that contained the gold. He found a small ledge overhanging the rocks. Walt ducked and crawled under the ledge and moved over to make room for Barb. She followed close behind.

With a rock ledge over their heads, they had a measure of protection against whoever was shooting at them from the helicopter. The trouble with their situation was, they had to stay where they were. They were trapped.

10

B rock finished his lunch off with a Lime Margarita. He had fresh fish with bananas, taro root, and taro leaves. He found the dish delicious. Pushing away from the table at the Blue Pearl Restaurant, he strode to the railing separating the restaurant from the beach. He decided to try Walt's number one more time. The call went straight to voice mail. Brock stared toward the ocean while thinking about the call. Walt not answering his phone seemed very unusual. As field producer, Walt expected calls at all times of the day and night. On occasion, the calls were a matter of life and death.

Brock decided to go talk to the clerk at the front desk of Walt's hotel again. The first thing he did was to stop at the small store in the hotel lobby. The store served as a type of convenience store, charging highly inflated prices for common items. Earlier in the morning, Brock noticed the clerk smoking outside the door behind the front desk.

Brock purchased two packs of cigarettes and a small butane lighter. He opened one pack and threw out a few of the cigarettes. He stuffed both packs in his pockets and with one cigarette in his hand, he strolled up to the front desk with a smile.

The clerk greeted Brock with an equally charming smile.

Brock played with the cigarette in his hand as he asked, "How are things now, my friend?"

The clerk replied in a friendly voice, "Things are going good. It is a long day is all."

"Yes, you spend a lot of time here, don't you?"

"I do," the clerk said, "but I don't mind. This is a very good job."

Brock nodded his agreement and began to tell the clerk about some of the places he'd been. He spoke about how some men had trouble finding jobs and could not feed their families. Brock even made up things. He talked about poverty in places he'd never been. All the while, he played with the cigarette. Once, he even placed it in his mouth letting it dangle while he talked. Finally, Brock took the cigarette out of his mouth and said, "I'm going for a smoke, want to come along?"

The clerk smiled. "Yes, sure. Just allow me to prepare the desk for my absence."

Preparing the desk meant placing a small sign that said, *Ring bell for service,* on the desk. With that done and the desk tidied up, the clerk showed Brock out the rear door.

Brock shook another cigarette out of the pack and offered it to the clerk. When he took it, Brock lit his cigarette and pretended to inhale. He was a nonsmoker and he had a hard time not blanching at the smell. While they smoked, Brock struck up a conversation with the clerk.

They chatted about life on the island, money, and various other topics. Brock took out the pack of cigarettes and flipped it to the clerk. Showing him the full pack he still had, Brock said, "There, you can have that pack. I have another full pack."

The thankful clerk smiled. Soon they were back to chatting again. Before long, Brock brought the subject around to Walt. When they'd finished smoking, Brock learned everything the clerk knew about Walt.

Brock had a hunch something wasn't right. The desk clerk said he had not seen Walt or Barb since he had come on at seven a.m. Brock had never known Walt to stay inside a hotel room all day, even in the company of a woman. Tahiti was a tropical paradise. The Walt he knew would want to get out and enjoy the area. The clerk told Brock that Walt had inquired about a helicopter service and a dive shop. That sounded more like Walt. If he wasn't in his room, he must be diving somewhere among the outer islands.

Stubbing out the cigarette, Brock casually ended the conversation and drifted toward his room already formulating a plan of action. As soon as he got out of the hotel clerk's sight, he put his plan into action.

The helicopter hovered right over the rock outcrop at low altitude. The pilot brought the craft down so low the runners actually touched the tree tops. Walt and Barb squinted as the blades kicked up sand all around them.

After a moment, the pilot maneuvered the helicopter sideways, attempting to get the shooter in position for a better shot. The cockpit of the craft was slowly coming into view. Walt knew if he could see the cockpit, the man with the gun would be able to see him.

Suddenly, one of the blades of the helicopter caught one of the tree tops. Leaves and sticks flew, and the pilot pulled the craft up. He wrestled with the stick of the craft for a second before evening out. The helicopter hovered for a few more minutes, then turned away. Next, Walt and Barb heard it hovering over the short beach.

"Now what?" Barb asked.

"They're going to try to land on the beach. I'm not sure if there's enough room there." Walt thought the situation through. If the helicopter could land, the men would hunt them down. Walt and Barb only had knives for weapons. Faced with the prospect of fighting men with guns, he didn't think their chances were very good.

Only one solution came to mind. He took a deep breath, put his hands on Barb's shoulders, and looked her square in the eye. "I have a plan." He smiled and went on. "I'll have to go back and get one of the handguns."

"No way, Walt, you'll never make it."

"I could swim in, get a gun and swim back twice if I had to."

Barb insisted, "Walt, I'm serious."

"Listen, the only way this is going to work is if you stay away from them until I get the gun. Stay here for now. If you hear them coming, run for the other side of the island. Hold out as long as you can."

Barb stared at Walt. She didn't want to believe he would go back into that underwater deathtrap. If anyone could do it, she knew it would be Walt, but she wasn't sure anyone could do it. Putting on her bravest face, she said, "Hurry back."

Without a word, Walt turned and headed toward the beach. The helicopter hovered over the thin strand of sand beach forcing him to circle around and fight his way through the dense foliage. He hesitated when he got to the edge of the island. The bush ended where the gentle ocean waves rolled up to the bank. From here, Walt saw three men jump out of the helicopter as it hovered six feet above the surface of the sea. All three men carried rifles. One of the men came up limping from the hard landing. There wasn't enough room for the helicopter to land, so the pilot was forced to stay out away from the shore.

Walt eased out into the water up to his knees, before he bent at the waist and dove in. As he descended deeper underwater, he hoped he got into the sea unnoticed. He swam underwater until he reached the spot where he thought the entrance to the underground stream was located. Walt breached the surface of the sea barely creating a ripple. With only the top of his head above water, he looked back just in time to see the helicopter veer off and fly away from the beach. None of the men were anywhere in sight.

Walt inhaled three deep breaths of air. On the last one, he held his breath and dove for the bottom. Kicking hard, he got to the seafloor and swam for the rocky stream mouth. He found it right away and used strong strokes to make his way into the narrow rectangle tunnel. Walt turned on his light and adjusted it, so the beam shone straight ahead. The current wasn't strong, but it hindered his progress. He used a lot of energy to get to the narrow spot in the tubular tunnel.

Walt had thought the situation over in his head before he'd even gotten back in the water. The only chance he thought he'd have to squeeze through the tight spot, would be to exhale all his air. He hoped with his lungs empty, his chest would shrink enough to allow passage. The downside was, he'd have no air left. Once he expunged his air, he'd only have seconds until he needed to breathe.

The time for decision had come. As soon as Walt got to

the place where the rock constricted, he blew the air out of his lungs as he used his hands and arms to crawl along the narrow tunnel. With his air gone, he moved slowly through the streambed. His lungs began to burn. The walls and ceiling felt like they were closing in on him. Walt didn't let up. He continued clawing at the rock, pulling himself inch by inch along the tunnel.

For a moment, he thought he might be stuck, but when his foot found a hold against a jagged edge, it gave him the leverage to push himself forward and through the tight spot. The tunnel opened up on the other side and Walt frantically swam, pushed, and pulled himself along. Blood oozed from his fingers where he scraped the skin off. His knees were cut on the sharp rock. Walt saw the entrance to the large chamber just ahead. He knew the air tanks were laying on the floor right inside the entrance.

Walt willed himself to focus on one single thing, making it to the chamber. Nothing else mattered. Nothing else would matter if he didn't get to the air tanks. With his heart pounding and his lungs ready to explode, he reached the entrance to the chamber. Grabbing each side of the rock walls, he pulled himself inside as his vision began to go black. He had reached his threshold. Walt hit the stream floor and felt for the tanks. His hand brushed over one and Walt knelt beside it. With the last ounce of life he had left, he opened the regulator and fumbled with the mouthpiece until he got it in his mouth.

The feeling of relief as Walt sucked in great breaths of air calmed his rapid heart rate and restored his vision. He focused on slowing his breathing. Walt knew he'd been at the brink of pushing his body until it broke down. In a short time, his body returned to normal breathing. However, the strenuous activity started to take its toll. Walt wasn't sure he could get back through the streambed another time. He just didn't think he had it in him.

Forcing his mind to go over every detail of the cave where they found the gold, he tried to think of another way. He came up empty. Men with guns were hunting Barb at this very minute. He did not have time to explore other ways out but after a bit of thought, Walt did come up with an idea.

He pushed the mesh bag containing the guns into the tunnel first. Next, he filled his lungs with air before shoving the air tank into the tunnel. He would push these items along in front of him. When he got through the tight spot, he could use the tank for air and recover the guns.

The plan worked fine as Walt began to move along the volcanic tunnel to the constricted spot. He took a last breath from the air tank, then shoved it along with the mesh bag ahead. As he wiggled into the narrow spot, he blew the air out of his lungs. This time, the ordeal wasn't nearly as bad. The gentle current was enough to help Walt get through fairly fast. On the other side of the tight spot, he pushed the tank and bag ahead until they came out into the ocean fifteen-feet below the surface. When Walt swam out of the streambed, he found the mouthpiece, opened the air valve, and breathed in fresh air from the tank.

11

The sound of the helicopter grew distant as Barb picked her way along the faint trail from the outcrop to the far side of the atoll. She got to the edge of the water and saw the small island had no beach here. The bush came right up to the water's edge. Barb started to follow a thin path along the edge of the water. She only covered a short distance when she came upon an outrigger canoe.

Another one of the primitive bows and quiver full of arrows lay in the canoe. She assumed the craft must have belonged to the late Ricardo Baez. Barb stopped and took a few moments to think. Although the canoe had paddles, she'd never out-paddle rifles, not to mention the helicopter. If she paddled away from the atoll, she'd be a sitting duck. However, maybe she could create a diversion.

Barb removed the bow and quiver of arrows and gave the canoe a shove out into the clear blue water. The seaworthy craft floated easily away from land. Hopefully, the diversion would buy her some time. She watched it for a moment before walking away with the bow and arrows in hand. Moving quietly Barb snuck along the edge of the island looking for an ambush spot. As she rounded a turn, a fallen tree came into view. The tree had a heavy trunk and thick brush grew up around its branches. The thick cover would provide the perfect place to hide and wait. She crawled over the trunk and sat with her back against another, smaller tree. With an arrow nocked and the bow in her lap, Barb settled in and waited.

Two Whitetip Reef Sharks drifted by as Walt filled his lungs and the blood vessels in his muscles with oxygen. Walt kept an eye on the pair. They looked as though they were curious enough to come in for a closer investigation. That's all he needed; aggressive sharks getting in the way. He decided to don the air tank. That would allow him to stay underwater instead of swimming at the surface until he got to land. He'd be able to keep an eye on the sharks and stay hidden from the men, although the gin clear water wouldn't provide much cover.

Once he got the harness untwisted and the air tank on his back, Walt fastened the mesh bag to his swim shorts. He stayed close to the bottom as he kicked his fins toward the atoll. As predicted, the sharks came in close for a look. Walt made a quick move and reached out with his arm. The super agile sharks spooked and turned on a dime. They continued to circle slowly, but Walt no longer thought they'd give him any trouble.

He surfaced slowly twenty yards from the beach. Only allowing his mask to break the surface, Walt could see one man sitting on the beach. The man held his right leg and rocked back and forth as if in pain. His rifle was lying by his side. Soft as a whisper, Walt slid below the surface and swam for land. Due to the clarity of the water, he had no chance of surprise. His best chance was from land. Walt didn't feel too concerned. He now possessed two handguns, and if the man gave him the slightest bit of trouble, he would not hesitate to use them.

The helicopter circled the small atoll several times. Barb knew the pilot was looking for her. She wished she could be like that girl in the movies and shoot it down with the bow, but she knew that was an unreasonable expectation. If she had to shoot the bow, it would be at close range.

After a few passes, the helicopter pulled back, circling from much farther away. Barb assumed the pilot wanted a better overview of the entire area. With the helicopter a good distance away, the noise level dropped. Barb waited, listening intently. After a minute, she heard men's voices. Before long, the voices grew louder, and she heard footsteps. They were coming.

Grabbing onto some branches that hung out over the shallow water, Walt pulled himself onto land. He crawled into the dense brush on his belly. When he felt certain the man on the beach couldn't see him, he removed the air tank and took one of the guns out of the mesh bag. Saltwater would surely damage the weapon, but it should not affect its operation within the next few hours. He checked the clip to make sure it was loaded. The gun held nine shots and all nine were in the clip. Walt worked the chamber loading one cartridge into the breech.

Walt took deliberate steps toward the beach. He moved with stealth, trying to remain silent, but he was also keenly aware of Barb's situation. He moved quickly, eating up the distance between himself and the other man in a matter of seconds. When he got close, he saw the man cock his head as he heard a sound, but it was too late, Walt was upon him.

Breaking into a full-out run, Walt charged through the last ten feet of brush, leaped over a downed tree, and landed next to the startled man on the beach. The man rose, but his injured leg hampered his mobility. Walt hammered him in the nose with the butt of the automatic hand gun. The blow sent the man sprawling with blood pouring from his nose. Before he had a chance to react, Walt had the short barrel of the gun pressed against his head. The man stared at his dripping wet attacker with wide eyes.

Walt didn't want to kill the man, but Barb's life was at stake and he could not allow this man to slow him down. Walt brought the gun down again on top of the man's head. The man dropped like a bag of bricks. Walt didn't know how bad he'd injured the man, but he didn't look like he'd be causing any trouble anytime soon. Not bothering to tie his hands, Walt picked up the rifle, an outdated M1, and started along the trail leading inland.

He got to the rocky outcrop only to find it deserted. He noticed the faint trail leading toward the opposite side of the island. Walt stuffed the handgun back into the mesh bag and eased along the trail with the rifle at the ready.

The men came into view at last. There were two of them and as Barb watched from her station behind the fallen tree, she could see them pointing out to sea. She knew they had spotted the canoe. Her ploy had worked in distracting her pursuers, but they were too far away for her to take advantage of the situation. She wasn't familiar with shooting the bow. At this range, she didn't think she'd have much chance of hitting her target. Besides, there were two of them. Even if she hit one with an arrow, the other one still had a rifle. Also, the poison tipped arrow didn't stop Walt in his tracks. He had fought on for a time even after being shot. She could expect the same result if she arrowed one of the men.

The only chance she had was to hide. The men spoke to each other for a moment. Barb could tell they were discussing the canoe. Finally, they turned and continued along the trail, right toward her hide. For a moment, Barb thought they'd walk right past, but at the last second, one of the men noticed something. He stood within an arm's reach. From her vantage point, Barb could make out all the features on his face. She followed his eyes to the sandy ground. Her footprints were plainly visible in the sand. The man followed their trail until he raised his head and stared directly at her.

Barb had the bow ready. From her crouched position, she drew the bow and let loose an arrow in one quick motion. The shaft ricocheted off two branches before sailing harmlessly through the brush. Before she could nock another arrow, the man grabbed the bow and yanked her right out over the tree trunk.

Barb landed on her stomach with a force so hard it knocked the wind out of her. She clutched her midsection as she fought for air. The man stepped down with his boot on her face forcing her head into the sand. Barb gasped for air, but didn't try to get up. She knew the man could use his boot to crush her head with little effort.

The men spoke in a language she couldn't understand,

but just from hearing their tone of voice, she knew they were proud. She suspected her capture would benefit these men greatly. From a distance, she heard the best sound she thought she could ever hear ... Walt's voice.

"Hey, you," he called.

When the men turned, Walt fired the rifle. He aimed at the man with his boot on Barb's head. Walt was moving fast and breathing hard. This caused the shot to go high and to the right. The bullet grazed the man's shoulder. Walt stopped running. He steadied himself and took aim at the second man.

The man didn't have enough reaction time. He was a sitting duck. Walt squeezed the trigger, and nothing happened. The World War Two era rifle had misfired. This gave the second man a chance to shoulder his own M1 rifle. As Walt took a step toward the cover of the foliage, the man fired. Walt flew backward as his body went limp and he dropped like a stone.

The man smiled widely and admired his shooting prowess. Barb screamed and started to come to her feet, but the first man nailed the back of her head with the butt of his rifle. Barb saw stars. She fell first to her knees, then to the ground. In a daze, she was vaguely aware of the man picking her up and throwing her over his shoulder. As the man began walking, she heard him ask in English, "What about her friend?"

The second man said, "Don't worry about him, he is as dead as a doorknob."

Barb felt her stomach turn just before she passed out.

Brock McGowen decided to rent a car. With the help of the

desk clerk, he had a compact rental delivered to the hotel. Once he got his wheels, he went to the dive shop first. He spoke to the manager through one of his employees who spoke English. Though the translation came through a bit rough, Brock understood the basic story. Walt and Barb had rented dive gear and hired an experienced guide. They planned on diving a small atoll about twenty miles from Tahiti. They rented equipment for a standard reef dive. He didn't know when they would return, only that Walt paid extra so that the rental fee covered the whole day.

Brock made a note of the atoll's location and set off for his next stop, the helicopter service.

A burly man with a tattoo of a spear and a scroll on his neck was there to greet Brock as he got out of the car. The man eyed Brock with a suspicious gaze. Brock's senses went on alert immediately. He'd spent enough time around unsavory characters to know this man was dangerous.

The man strode toward Brock with threatening body language. Brock weighed the situation. The burly man had no reason to distrust Brock, or to interact with him in a threatening manner. From Brock's vast experience with this kind of situation, he made a quick determination.

The burly man stepped right up to him and stuck his face within an inch of Brock. Standing nose to nose, he could almost feel the anger from the man boiling over. Brock stared at the burly man with a passive look on his face. He knew what he was going to do. He didn't talk. He didn't blink. He didn't take a step back, but held his ground. With a quickness that had fooled more than one man, Brock brought his knee up into the man's groin.

The man grunted and doubled over. Brock struck fast with a blow to the side of his head. The blow landed right below where the man's jutting jaw met his neck. The open-handed blow wasn't meant to do any real damage, but merely to incapacitate the aggressor.

Dropping on his knees to the pavement, the man grunted. Brock made a quick adjustment, grabbed the man's arm, and twisted his thumb backward.

"Ah!" the man cried. "Get off me."

"Where are they?"

The man struggled. Brock knew he didn't want to give up any information, but he also knew he wouldn't want his thumb broken either. He increased the pressure.

Again, the man gasped. "Ah, you are breaking my thumb. Stop!"

Brock gave it a little more pressure before easing off just a bit. "Tell me where they are right now, or I'll permanently disable your thumb." The truth was, Brock didn't know if the thumb would be disabled permanently, but he knew he could do a lot of damage and cause a great deal of pain.

"Who are you?"

"Where is the helicopter?" Brock answered with his own question.

"It's out on a tour."

"Where?"

"I do not know. Out over the islands somewhere."

"Walter Ulrich. Where did the helicopter take Walter Ulrich?"

Sweat beaded up on the man's forehead. His mouth quivered as he answered, "I do not know. One of the small leeward islands."

"Why did you come at me like that?"

After a short hesitation, the man said, "I am not supposed to allow anyone near the hangar. I do not know the full situation."

"When did they leave?"

The man made an attempt to break free. Like a dog can sense fear, Brock knew something was up. He had little patience for a petty test of wills. When the man wriggled and tried to gain leverage, Brock pulled back hard on his thumb. With a sharp crack, the bone broke, and the man screamed. Releasing his grip on the thumb, Brock grabbed the man's pinky and twisted it back. He now had the same leverage on the pinky as he previously had on the thumb.

"When did the helicopter leave," Brock repeated in a calculated tone.

The burly man hung his head. From the sound of Brock's voice and his sheer ruthlessness, he understood Brock would not stop at anything to get what he wanted.

"You're in a tough spot, but you might as well save your fingers. You have a long life ahead of yourself," Brock said, trying to convince the man to see things his way.

"The helicopter left first thing this morning."

"What about Walter Ulrich?"

"They took him out on a tour yesterday. All I know is that they came back without him."

"Why would they do that?"

The man said, "That is all I know. I am not in high standing with this company. I do not know all the things that go on here."

Brock shoved the man and walked back to the car. As he pulled away from the helicopter pad, the man was still on his knees staring at his damaged thumb.

He drove to the docks next. When he arrived, he pulled over to the side and called the front desk clerk at the hotel. He asked for and received directions to the island where the helicopter supposedly took Walt and Barb.

With a million and one scenarios running through his head, Brock walked to the docks to charter a boat.

12

_____

Everything looked fuzzy when Walt opened his eyes. He blinked, and his vision cleared the slightest bit, although he couldn't piece together what he saw. He took a deep breath and pain erupted in his head. Walt wanted to stand. Instead, he stayed still and tried to remember what had happened.

An underground stream came to mind. He remembered swimming . . . and Barb was there too. Barb, the name brought back more memories. Where was she now? Why would she have been swimming in an underground stream by his side? He had no answers. Walt lay still and inhaled a few deep breaths. Slowly, he felt his mind clear and he regained his memory. Within five minutes, he remembered everything.

The most vivid recollection he had, was of trying to dive out of the way and having a man shoot at him. He picked up the shattered rifle that he had in his hands when the shot was fired. From the way he held the rifle when he dove, the angle of the shot drove into the hard, wooden stock right behind the trigger. The force of the shot slammed the stock against Walt's head knocking him unconscious. The bullet deflected and didn't hit Walt at all. He knew he was one lucky customer. But then he remembered Barb.

Walt got up on one knee. With a huge amount of effort, he pushed off and rose to his feet. His head spun for a quick second, but the feeling quickly faded, and he felt OK. He gazed at his surroundings and saw no sign of Barb or the men with the rifles. Walt remembered hearing one of them say he was dead and he vaguely recalled them leaving with Barb. He had to find her, but in his physical condition, he didn't know if he could do much of anything. Walt walked over to where he'd last seen Barb. Signs of a scuffle were evident, and a few spots of blood decorated the sandy ground.

Walt searched for clues to tell him what had happened to Barb. He found nothing to suggest she'd been killed. Walt felt certain Barb had been taken off the island alive, but he had more questions than answers.

After a quick search of the immediate area, he set out and searched the entire island. The more Walt moved, the better he felt. His head cleared completely, and he regained his normal sharp thoughts. He found nothing of help on the island. The man he cold cocked with his handgun was gone along with the other two men and Barb.

Walt took inventory of his belongings. For weapons, he still had both handguns, his knife, and the crude bow and arrows Ricardo had left. He had one air tank and regulator, a dive light, and his swim fins so he could make a dive if he needed to. The handcrafted raft was still in its place under the brush, although Walt didn't think it would float for very much longer.

That was it. He had meager supplies, but he'd have to make do. The real problem he faced was not knowing where the men had taken Barb and why. There were a large number of miniscule atolls in the region. Searching them one at a time would take too long. Walt needed an edge. He needed to know exactly where Barb was.

Returning to the rocky outcrop, he appraised the sealed entrance. With his background in mining, Walt had an eye for excavating blocked earthworks. The boulders blocking the entrance way were large, and from the inside, they were almost impossible to move. The main reason being, there were no tools inside. Out here, Walt could use some of the island's natural resources to solve the problem.

With the sun sinking low, Walt got to work. Out of a tree trunk cut from the dense brush, he fashioned a long pole to use as a lever. Using some ingenuity, he built a small fulcrum. Walt used the leverage of the long pole to move rocks one by one. When the sun sank, and it got too dark to see, he strapped the dive light to his head and worked into the night.

Brock found it impossible to rent a boat. None of the local fishermen or tour guides wanted anyone taking their boat. In this part of the world, boats were their bread and butter. He didn't blame the locals. Allowing a stranger to rent your boat was never a sensible idea and he would not go for it either if he wore their shoes. The problem was, he felt certain Walt and Barb were in some kind of trouble. In the end, he found a man willing to sell, so he bought a boat outright. Brock paid twice what it was worth, but he got a good, dependable boat in the deal.

When he finally got everything straightened out, it was late afternoon. He decided to go out anyway. If Walt and

Barb had been involved in an accident, it might be too late, or . . . every second could count. Brock planned on searching one or two islands this evening. While the seller of the boat removed his personal items, Brock grabbed some food and drinks thinking maybe he'd stay out overnight and resume the search in the morning. With a full tank of gas, a few sandwiches, and some bottled water, Brock set out for the small atoll the burly man said Walt might have flown to. He hoped he could make it before dark. Looking at the horizon, he also hoped the dark clouds forming would turn in a different direction.

Every time Walt moved one rock out of the way, more fell to take its place. This was the nature of the beast. Walt knew he had to remove all the loose debris from the entrance to make it safe enough to go through. Piece by piece, he moved earth from the entrance. Eventually, he broke through the wall of rock and dirt. When he stuck a branch into the entrance, he could feel it go through the thin layer and into the empty chamber.

Doubling his efforts, Walt tore at the rocks sealing off the opening. An hour later, he had a hole big enough to crawl through. When Walt got into the large outer room on his hands and knees, he instantly smelled the stale air. While the entrance was sealed, there had been no airflow. Fresh air began to circulate now that there was a hole in the closure. The first thing he did was to go to the stream of fresh water and drink. The cool water soothed his scorched throat and reinvigorated Walt. When he'd drank his fill, he shined his light around the room until he found the map. Walt spent a long time examining the islands along with the markings on the map. He thought he knew which atoll was marked on the map. The one which he had seen the man paddling toward earlier in the day appeared to have the most importance. Walt did not know for certain if Barb had been taken to that particular island, but he figured it would be a good place to start.

His next consideration was how to get there? He could barely make out the speck of land in the daylight. Walt didn't think the raft would float nearly half that far. He could attempt to swim, but that would be a long shot. The best idea he could come up with was to repair the raft and make it seaworthy enough to make the trip.

Thunder rolled in the distance. Walt pondered the situation for a long while. His body and mind had taken a heck of a beating over the two days. His relaxing South Sea vacation had turned into a constant struggle for survival, and the end was nowhere in sight. That last thought planted a seed in his head. Walt knew the men who had Barb thought he was dead, and he believed that would work to his advantage. Now, he wasn't so sure. He didn't know how he could manage it, but what if he could lure the abductors here, to this atoll?

As rain began to fall, he decided there wasn't much he could do in the dark. The beam of his dive light began to grow faint, so he turned it off to save the battery. Alone in the cave, Walt sat with his back against the hard rock wall and drifted off to a much-needed sleep.

Late evening found Brock cruising the outer atolls. First, he searched a tiny spit of land that produced nothing. An hour boat ride brought him to the second coral atoll. Anchoring the boat in the calm lagoon, Brock waded through the warm water to the beach. A quick scan of the area revealed discouraging signs. The disturbance in the sand on the beach showed definite signs of a helicopter landing. From what Brock saw, it looked as though the helicopter landed more than once in the past few days.

A plethora of footprints cluttered the beach. Most were made from work or military type boots. However, mixed in were prints of bare feet along with a few that looked as though they were made by someone wearing swim fins. With the approaching storm bearing down in his direction, Brock knew he didn't have much time to decipher tracks and footprints. In another hour or so, the storm would probably wash away all evidence of human activity.

The prints led Brock to a narrow path that entered the brush. The path had seen a good deal of activity lately. Brock followed the winding trail to a spot where something had disturbed a wide area of sandy soil. When Brock knelt, he saw what looked like blood mixed in the sand. He stood and examined the spot. A picture formed in his mind of something or someone dead laying here. It looked to Brock as though an effort was made to clean the area up. With a feeling of despair growing in the pit of his stomach, he continued along the trail.

Brock followed the trail and found his way to the abandoned shack. After he inspected the dwelling and its contents, Brock felt certain Walt and Barb had been in the shack. He found a bloody T-shirt he thought belonged to Walt and noticed small footprints and a small handprint in the sand. He believed they were made by Barb Kendall. The million-dollar question was, where were they?

Brock spent another hour combing the atoll for any clue that might lead him to the whereabouts of his friends. As darkness closed in, he stopped searching, confident in the belief he'd done everything he could have to discover clues.

The wind picked up and the first drops of rain began to fall as Brock waded back out to the anchored boat. He would spend the night here on the boat and resume his search in the morning. He ate a supper of two sandwiches and washed them down with bottled water in the cozy cabin while the storm battered the boat.

The storm didn't last long. For forty minutes the wind raged, and heavy rain fell, but the worst of the storm passed, and things began to settle. An hour after the first rain began to fall, the nighttime sky turned clear and bright. Brock went out onto the deck, cracked open a bottle of beer and stared at the stars. He pondered the situation, hoping to find insight to where Walt and Barb could be and what kind of shape they'd be in when he did find them. For all he knew, they might not even still be alive. He put that thought out of his head as quickly as it entered. Born from surviving a bevy of nerve-wracking, do-or-die situations, Brock knew maintaining a positive attitude would be key to any success.

The storm had whipped up waves, but now the surface of the sea calmed to a gentle swell that worked to lull Brock into a relaxed state. He took another pull on the bottle of beer more to stay awake then for any other reason. In a short time, he felt his eyes growing heavy and his head began to drop as he nodded off.

A muffled thump caught his attention. He tuned in to the sounds of the night, listening with intense interest. Brock heard the dwindling breeze and the soft lapping of the waves against the hull of the boat. He didn't hear anything else. In his relaxed state, Brock second-guessed whether he heard a noise at all.

Then, he heard it again. Something bumped against the

hull and it wasn't a gentle wave, it sounded like a solid object. Brock downed another swallow of beer. He flipped the bottle, so he held it by the neck and crouched beside the doorway to the cabin. The last drop of beer spilled onto the deck.

Soon, he felt the boat list to the port side. Brock's eyes narrowed when he saw a man crawl over the gunwale. The bare-chested and barefoot man held a deadly looking knife in one hand and sported a menacing look on his face. The scene reminded Brock of the islanders coming aboard the boat to capture the heroine in the movie *King Kong*.

The intruder stepped lightly to the entryway to the cabin, no doubt thinking he had been undetected. As he reached for the door, Brock whacked him over the head with the beer bottle. The bottle smashed against the man's hard skull and sent him to the deck. Brock relieved him of his knife and silently tread to the gunwale. He peered over the side and saw a small canoe tied to the stern of his boat.

Satisfied that the intruder had worked alone, he went back to where the man lay in a spreading pool of blood. Brock hunkered on his haunches and said, "Now look at the mess you made. I just bought this boat you know." He lifted the man by his black, curly hair, noticing the tattoo on his neck. The spear and scroll tattoo matched the one the burly man at the helicopter service had. "And even worse than that, you made me waste the last of my beer. There was still a swallow left in that bottle."

13

—————

Water splashed against his skin and went up his nose. The man found himself tied to a chair in the cabin of the very boat he boarded earlier in an attempt to kill its owner. Brock stared at the intruder with disdain. Although a stream of blood still trickled down the side of his head, he felt little pity for the man who would have killed him. Brock knew many islanders lived meager lives well below what was considered the poverty line, but when it came to kill or be killed, he always wanted to be on the winning side.

As the man came around, he struggled at his restraints to no avail. Brock secured his hands and feet with knots that would get tighter the more he struggled against them. Lowering his head so his face came within an inch of the bound man's face, Brock said, "You have about one minute to tell me where my friends are. If you refuse, I'll kill you and dump you over the side, then I'll go after the rest of your group. I'm going to find them one way or another, so you might as well start talking."

Brock's threatening speech went over like a lead balloon.

The man stared back at him with a confident smirk. Brock tried several more threats and each produced similar results. Nothing. The man had no intention of giving up one iota of information, and Brock had no intention of torturing or killing the man. The confrontation had come to a standstill.

He didn't know what to do with the trespasser, so Brock made sure he couldn't escape and left him in the cabin. Brock knew he'd gotten lucky this time. If he would not have heard the small canoe bump against the hull, he didn't believe he'd be here to think about it. He wasn't about to sit around waiting for another attacker to come slinking aboard in the night.

Firing up the engines, Brock put the boat in gear and headed out to sea. He'd anchor, or maybe just let her drift until dawn, then resume his search paying little attention to what happened or the prisoner he held in the cabin. There would be time for those things later. Tomorrow, he would hunt for Walt and Barb.

———

Walt roused from his slumber before the first rays of sun painted the horizon. In the dark he used his dive light and made his way to the beach and the raft. He spent over an hour repairing and strengthening the jumbled mass of poles, leaves, and rope. When the sun had risen, he was ready. Walt shoved the raft down the sandy beach and into the ocean. The plank paddles were still on the raft. With the spear gun, two handguns, and his dive knife, Walt paddled for the distant atoll.

———

When the morning sky turned pink in the east, Brock started the engines. He decided to make the next closest atoll his next stop. He didn't sleep a wink all night, and he felt glad when the dawn brought enough light to resume the search.

He circled the tiny piece of land before settling on a small sand beach for the landing. He brought the bow of his newly acquired boat right up on the sand and beached her. Brock hopped over the side and fastened the bow line to a scrubby tree. He used the boarding ladder on the stern to crawl back into the boat. Brock had a few loose ends to take care of before he started his search of the atoll. He wanted to take some supplies along and make certain his prisoner couldn't escape in his absence. When he entered the cabin, he found the man struggling violently with his bindings. He had a look of utter fear in his eyes and on his face. The man was terrified.

"What's wrong with you?" Brock asked, a trace of amusement in his voice.

"We must leave now. Right away! Please, we cannot stay here."

Brock realized something had changed. He crouched close to the man. "What is it? What are you afraid of?"

The man trembled. "We must get away from this island right away."

"Tell me what's going on," Brock demanded.

"This island is haunted. Guarded by an ancient Tapu."

"Yea, well whatever."

"Please, before you set foot on that cursed island, set me free. You will not be coming back, and I do not want to die tied up aboard your boat," the man pleaded.

Brock headed for the companionway to the back deck. "Maybe I could give you your knife back too. You remember your knife don't you, the one you tried to kill me with?"

The man began to mutter something under his breath. To Brock it sounded like a chant or a prayer. Brock had always been a practical man and he had heard enough of this man's ghost stories. He stuffed the knife in his waistband and waded to shore. Just as there were tell-tale signs left on the beach of the other atoll, this beach had also seen recent activity. From the disturbance in the sand, he felt certain some type of struggle took place there. With extreme caution, Brock eased along the trail deeper into the brush.

At the rocky outcrop, Brock saw the footprints going in and out of the narrow crack in the otherwise solid formation. With the knife at the ready, he poked his head inside, however he found it too dark to see anything. Brock backed out and continued his search of the island. On the far side he found more signs of a struggle and a few dried drops of blood. The island was uninhabited, so Brock returned to the boat for a flashlight. Something was in that cavern and he was going to find out what it was.

Barb woke to find herself in a small thatched hut. Her hands and feet were bound, and she was tied to a pole in the center of the hut. Her clothes had been removed and she now wore traditional Polynesian dress consisting of a cloth skirt and a top made of palm leaves and strips of bark. At least something covered her top. Polynesian women in ancient times only wore skirts and were usually bare-chested.

Although she was barefoot, the bandage was in place on her wounded thigh. Confusion clouded her mind. She could not imagine why she would be dressed this way. The natural sounds of the island such as birds chirping and calling was the only noise she heard. From the light filtering in through the cracks in the walls of the hut, Barb knew it was daytime.

Her head ached, and she could not remember anything since the shootout. She did not know if it was the same day or if several days had passed. The thoughts of Walt being shot and killed saddened her deeply. However, Barb's sadness quickly turned to anger. Walt might be gone, but she swore under her breath she'd make his killers pay, even if it was the last thing she ever did. After a minute of struggling against her restraints, Barb settled down and relaxed. Whoever had captured her wanted her alive for a reason. She wasn't going to be able to break free, but she knew eventually someone would come into the hut. She needed her wits about her. Barb planned to bide her time and strike at the right moment.

When Brock retrieved the flashlight from the boat he paid little attention to the unintelligible ranting coming from the man who'd tried to kill him. The man rocked back and forth in the chair muttering and moaning and making no sense.

Now, as he shone the light into the dark crevice, he wondered what could frighten a man to that degree. With a trace of trepidation, he moved into the chamber. Brock shone his light around the room before his beam settled on the table with the tablet. With slow, careful movements, he moved deeper inside the cavern.

Brock took his time and spent a few minutes reading the journal. He found the story amazing and because he knew Walt for a good many years, he felt certain this all had something to do with his disappearance. If there was a hidden treasure within a hundred-mile radius, Walt would find it.

When he finished reading Brock moved toward the second chamber. The gold coins scattered on the stone floor between chambers made his heart rate increase. As he flicked his light around the piles and piles of gold in the second chamber, his heart rate went through the roof. When he regained a semblance of control, Brock remarked, "Well, what do you know, a hidden treasure."

14

W alt dipped the plank paddle in the water, pulled, and stroked at a steady pace. Once he got away from the island, he could feel only a trace of crosscurrent running against the raft. He'd gotten almost halfway and although his gains were slow, the raft had held up just fine. A pair of dolphins playing close to the surface attracted Walt's attention. The pair frolicked and swam fifty yards from where he paddled across the reach between the islands.

Walt didn't notice the sound of the boat until it bore down on him from three-hundred yards away. He turned his head and saw a cabin cruiser planning over the chop at a high rate of speed. He stopped paddling and stared at the approaching boat. As it closed the distance, several things became apparent. The operator of the boat wasn't friendly, and the boat wasn't about to stop. On its present course it would run right over him.

Walt didn't have much time to react. Paddling away from the fast boat would not work. His weapons would be his only chance, and he'd have to have a degree of luck if he was going to get out of this alive. He maneuvered the raft sideways just to see what the boat would do. As predicted, the boat adjusted its course and came straight at him. Walt didn't have time to hesitate. He tried to steady himself as best he could on the unstable, rocking raft, aimed a handgun, and fired. The first bullet flew high. Walt pulled the trigger again and again with no visible results.

When the gun was empty, he dropped it and picked up the second handgun, however he was out of time. The boat came on like a freight train. Walt dove off the raft and to the side at the last second and a split second ahead of the bow of the boat crashing into the raft. The fiberglass hull bumped his legs and dragged him under. The handgun dropped from his hand as Walt fought to reorient himself and swim away from the boat. From twelve feet under water, Walt watched the boat pass over and head away before slowing and making a wide turn. His worse fear came to fruition. The boat was coming back and in this gin clear water he'd be a sitting duck with nowhere to hide.

From inside the cavern the muffled sound of the engine sounded distant. Several moments went by until Brock realized the sound was coming from right outside. He looked up from the map and cocked his head listening. The sound grew quieter. In an instant Brock realized the noise was coming from his boat. He hurried from the cavern and sprinted along the short trail back to the beach. When he reached the beach, his boat was gone.

"I'll be damned," Brock swore.

Although he couldn't see the boat, he could still hear the engine. Brock spun on his heels and took off for the far side of the island at a run. Following the trail, he passed the rocky outcrop and ended up on the far side of the island in time to see the boat headed toward another distant atoll. A small canoe trailed the boat. The canoe was tied off to the stern of the boat and swung wildly in its wake. With his hands on his hips, Brock shook his head in anger. An accomplice must have snuck onto the boat and freed the man who Brock had held in captivity. Although he could not perceive what the object was, he noticed something else far out in the water. He shielded his eyes with his hand on his forehead and stared hard at the blue Pacific. His thirty-eight-year-old eyes did not deceive him. A dark speck in the water confirmed his thoughts. Something was out there.

Not wanting to risk surfacing and getting plowed over by the oncoming boat, Walt decided retrieving the handgun would be the best course of action. He saw the gun fall toward the bottom and had a rough idea where it was, but from ten feet off the bottom, he could not actually see the gun. Blowing out some of the air in his lungs to make diving easier, Walt swam for the seafloor. Although the ocean water was clear, his visibility was limited without goggles. Everything looked blurry and slightly distorted.

When he reached the seabed, Walt began scanning the bottom for the gun. The amplified sound from the boat engine increased and Walt looked up to see the boat coming straight on. When it reached his position, the engine was cut back, and the boat idled on the swells directly above him. Walt knew he was in deep trouble. He had not found the gun, and even if he could, he would still have to surface and shoot it out with whoever was aboard the boat. He'd be winded when he surfaced, and his eyes would still be blurry. Walt didn't like the odds of that scenario.

He continued to scour the seafloor although his heart rate increased, and his lungs began to ache. Just when he was ready to give up and swim for the surface, Walt saw the air tank standing on end, protruding straight up from the bottom. He swam to where the tank lay, shoved the mouthpiece into his mouth, and opened the regulator. Walt inhaled a deep breath and forced himself to relax. He wasn't sure how much air remained in the tank, but for now it provided some extra time underwater and out of harm's way.

Slipping into the harness, Walt donned the air tank and scanned his surroundings. The boat still floated directly above him. Not much plant life grew on the seafloor. He thought he should be able to find the gun without too much trouble, but as he began to search Walt heard a splash on the surface. Looking up, Walt saw a man swimming for the bottom. The man wore swim fins, a snorkel, and dive goggles. In one hand he held a spear. Walt watched and waited. The man saw him and started swimming directly toward where he hunched down on the bottom.

When the man drew close, Walt got a better look at the spear. The carbon-based shaft was about six feet in length and the barbed tip looked razor-sharp. The spear was the style used before modern band and pneumatic spear guns were invented. To this day, some divers still chose to use the traditional spears.

Walt remained patient as the man swam steadily toward him. He crouched and when the man got close enough, he sprang off the bottom and grabbed the shaft of the spear. Walt slammed into the man and although the maneuver surprised his foe, he instantly found himself in a deadly struggle. While Walt tried to pry the spear from his hand, the man produced a knife in his free hand. Walt used his arm to deflect a blow aimed at his neck. He heard the tip of the blade scrape against his air tanks as the knife missed its mark.

Walt released his grip on the spear and focused on the knife. With both hands he smashed the man's hand down against the bottom. The knife dropped from his hand, but he used the shaft of the spear to hit Walt hard on the back of his head. The blow made Walt see stars and sent a wave of pain through his head. He involuntarily let go of the spear. The man adjusted the spears position in his hands and thrust the tip at Walt's midsection. Twisting to the side and pushing the shaft away, Walt felt the edge of the pointed tip slip by to the side of his ribs. The blade barely nicked his side and opened up a small, shallow cut about two inches long.

Reacting with lightning speed, Walt drove his fist into the man's jaw. The water slowed the punch, but it still carried enough energy to snap the man's head back. Walt went right for the spear, but the other man was too quick. He had the distinct advantage of wearing swim fins. This made him quicker and more agile underwater. He also wore goggles which allowed him to see more clearly. However, Walt had scuba gear, while the man only wore a snorkel. If all else failed, he could try to keep the man submerged until he ran out of air.

The man twisted the spear from Walt's grasp and thrust again, this time the point of the spear was aimed at his head. Walt moved away with ease, then grabbed the man from behind in a bear hug. The air tank made him heavier than his opponent and he used his weight to force the man to the seafloor. The man kicked and squirmed, but Walt held on for dear life keeping him pinned to the bottom. Walt saw the man expel all the air from his lungs. He knew the next action would be for the man to inhale. Walt wasn't a killer, but this man had tried to take his life. He also believed the man had something to do with Barb's disappearance. Walt held on without regret. The man struggled harder, but soon went rigid as he inhaled a great gasp of seawater. He fought on for a bit longer. Eventually, he weakened and eventually became still.

Walt relaxed and released his grip on the drowned man. His relief did not last long. When he attempted to inhale a breath, he found his air tank empty. That was one bad feature of scuba gear. The apparatus gave no warning, when the air was gone, it was gone. Now, Walt found himself on the seafloor with someone waiting to kill him at the surface and very little oxygen in his lungs. He didn't have time to wait. Prying the spear from the dead man's hands, Walt kicked hard and swam for the surface. He figured he'd only have one chance and silently vowed to make it count.

Walt broke the surface and saw the man on the boat at the same instant. Through cloudy, waterlogged eyes he saw the man leaning along the side of the boat. Walt propelled himself as far out of the water as he could and threw the spear. He aimed for the man's head, but the spear sailed to the right and missed by three inches.

The vicious attack startled the man and he fell backward onto the deck. By the time he clambered back to his feet, Walt was beginning to climb over the side of the boat. The man punched Walt in the face, then kicked him back into the water. His eyes were wild, and panic tugged at the man's mind. He could not understand how this Devil could have survived the attack by his partner. Now the Devil was coming after him. He ran to the controls, threw the transmission in gear, and pushed the throttle to its stops.

The bow of the boat lifted out of the water as it lurched forward. Walt breathed in a nose full of water from the wave created by the hull of the boat as it sped away. Treading water and coughing, he watched as the boat turned for the distant atoll, the one where he thought Barb might be held.

Once again, Walt found himself alone in the water. The slight current ran across and slightly back toward where he'd come from. He was less than halfway to his destination. The raft had been destroyed. With no raft, and nothing to hold onto to help stay afloat, Walt didn't think he could make it to the atoll. With a defeated sigh, he turned and started swimming back to the island he'd come from.

15

Brock stared at the thing in the water, but from this distance he couldn't make out what it was. He quickly dismissed it as a marine animal of some type and allowed his gaze to follow the boat, which now looked like little more than a speck. The boat was headed straight for the far-off atoll. From this distance the atoll looked like little more than a low smudge on the horizon. Brock had no way of knowing how big it was, if it was inhabited, or anything else about the spit of land in the distance. One thing he had brought along from the boat was his satellite phone. The signal was spotty, but he thought he had a fifty-fifty chance of getting a call through. The question was, who would he call? Barb and Walt were out here somewhere and after the events of the past two days, he didn't trust anyone on the island except possibly the front desk clerk at the hotel.

He stood staring out to sea and thinking about his situation for a few moments. Then, he remembered the map in the cavern. Maybe he could determine something about the distant atoll from the map. With a last glance out to sea, he turned and started back along the trail toward the outcrop.

"You know, I've spent my life around the islands of the Caribbean, but the stunning beauty of this place is unmatched," Lynn Smith remarked. Gazing out the window from the cockpit of the single engine Beechcraft Bonanza airplane, she continued, "It's not so much that the South Pacific is vastly different from the Caribbean, but this area is so remote."

From his seat at the controls of the light aircraft, her husband Denny Smith agreed, "It sure is remote. Even today with internet and satellites and all the modern forms of transportation, these islands and the waters around them are like wilderness."

Lynn nodded. "Even though I'm six months pregnant," she patted her ample stomach before continuing, "I'm glad we took this vacation now. It might be awhile before we can do something like this again."

"Me too. The boys are going to be surprised," Denny said in agreement, referring to Walt and Brock.

When Brock spoke to Denny on the phone earlier in the week, he mentioned heading to Tahiti for a short vacation. The idea of taking a vacation with his wife sprouted from that conversation. The fact that Walter Ulrich was already here made the thought of the trip even more enticing. Spanish Pirates and Mexican drug gangs were a few of the adversaries he'd faced on various adventures with Walt and Brock. He considered Walter Ulrich and Brock McGowen the best friends he had and looked forward to seeing them again.

"You don't think they know we're coming?" asked Lynn.

Denny banked the plane before straightening out as he

passed over a small atoll. "No way. It will be a big surprise and I know they'll enjoy flying around the islands."

Lynn smiled as she gazed at the turquoise South Pacific water and the green and white of the atoll which stood out in stark contrast. "I agree with you on that one. Who wouldn't enjoy this?"

The couple had taken a commercial flight into Fa' a' a International Airport, Tahiti's main connection with the outside world. From there, they rented a nineteen-sixty Beech Craft plane. The engine had been overhauled and after close inspection, Denny deemed the plane in tip-top condition.

Their plan was to travel to Tahiti and surprise Walt and Brock. They'd spend the week relaxing in the warm Pacific water and exploring the area in the rented plane.

Denny motioned toward the horizon. As Denny banked the plane, the island of Tahiti came into view once again. Both Denny and Lynn marveled at the magnificent volcanic mountains that rose seemingly out of the sea. Lush green vegetation covered the steep slopes almost to their peaks where craggy grey rock replaced any foliage. Wisps of mist floated by the dormant volcanoes giving the island a mysterious mystique. Thin rivers cascaded off the edges of the mountains in stunning waterfalls. Years of recreational flying prior to owning a flight school had worked to make Denny Smith an above average pilot. Denny radioed the airfield and after receiving permission to land, brought the Beech Craft down for a smooth landing.

"Let the relaxation begin!" Denny announced as he brought the plane to a stop.

If there was one thing Walt did best, swimming had to be it. From his days in an Atlantic City, New Jersey pool to the swim team at Rutgers University, Walt always excelled in the water. Now he used precise strokes to propel himself through the water. He had no doubt he could swim the distance to the atoll with little trouble, but sharks were always a concern. Putting the thought out of his mind, he continued at a steady pace.

Almost a half hour after he'd started, Walt staggered up to the trail that ran along the edge of the small atoll. The strenuous action of the last several days had taken a toll on his body and he took a few seconds to catch his breath and regain his strength. When he was ready, he headed back along the trail toward the outcropping. As he approached, he heard a muffled sound from inside the opening. Barb was in trouble. Walt was going to find her, and he wouldn't allow anything, or anyone, to stand in his way. He had already ended several lives in a fight for his own survival. If he had to fight again, he'd be ready. Walt picked up a fist-sized rock and slipped into the crevice.

By the dim light of a flashlight, Walt saw a man hunched over the table in the center of the first chamber. As quietly as he could, he crept up behind the man and raised the rock. An instant before he was ready to slam the rock into the back of the other man's head, the man spun around and grabbed his arm with one hand and delivered a right cross with the other hand. The blow stunned Walt and knocked him flat on his back. Before he had a chance to react, the man was on top of him with his fist raised. Then he heard a familiar voice.

"Walt? Is that you?"

The right cross rang his bell pretty hard, and Walt shook his head trying to clear the cobwebs. He focused on the dimly lit face of the man on top of him. Although he could not actually discern who he was looking at, the shape of the face looked familiar and the voice certainly sounded like his old friend Brock McGowen. "Get off me," were the only words he could muster.

"It is you," Brock said, backing off and lowering his fist. "Man, I'm glad to see you."

"Brock?"

"The one and only. What's going on Walt? Where's Barb?"

Still trying to comprehend, Walt asked, "What are you doing here?"

Brock stood and extended his hand. When Walt took it, Brock helped his friend to his feet.

"I came for a vacation. I couldn't find hide or hair of you and Barb at any of the resorts, so I started snooping."

Walt rubbed his chin. "Something you're good at."

"And by the look of things, it's lucky for you I am good at it," Brock chided. "What's going on?"

"We took a helicopter tour to another atoll . . ."

"The one to the east," Brock interrupted.

"Yes, and as soon as we landed people were trying to kill us."

"Do you know who or why?"

"Not really, but I'm certain it has something to do with this treasure. Have you seen the treasure yet?"

Brock's face grew animated. "Oh yea, I saw it all right. There's an enormous fortune in that other room. This treasure makes the one we found in the Florida Keys look small."

As they stepped over to the map, Walt went over the details of their adventure from the time he dove with Pierre right up to Barb's capture.

"So, you think they have Barb on this atoll?" Brock asked, pointing to the speck of land on the map.

Walt looked thoughtful. "Well, there are no signs that she was killed anywhere on this island . . . no big pools of blood or anything. The islander we saw in the canoe yesterday was paddling in that direction. Now, the boat that came after me went directly toward that atoll. If she's alive, and I believe she is, I'm betting that's where she is."

"By the way," Brock said, "I own the boat that assaulted you. I bought it in Tahiti. A local guy snuck aboard last night, and I subdued him, but he must have had help. While I was in here, they stole my boat and that's when they found you."

"We need to find a way over to that atoll."

"And you really think this treasure has something to do with all this?"

"It's the only thing that makes any sense. I believe we were attacked by Ricardo Baez because he didn't want us to find the treasure. I also think these other men are trying to keep us from removing the treasure because of the curse or whatever it is."

Brock sighed. "We can slap together another raft or," he said, lifting his satellite phone from his pocket, "we can make some calls and buy another boat. I don't have signal in here, but outside I think I'll have enough to call Tahiti."

"I don't know what they're up to, or how long they'll keep Barb alive. Let's go make some calls."

Walt led the way out into the bright sunshine with Brock a step behind.

When they got to the small beach Brock took out his phone. "The problem is, I just don't know who to call. Should we call the police?"

Walt pondered the question for a moment. "From what I've seen, I don't trust anyone."

"The only person I know is the desk clerk at your hotel. I could try to get him to get us a boat out here."

Walt shook his head. "No, that would take too long. He'd have to find a boat for sale, somehow buy it using your funds, then make arrangements to get it to our location." Walt thought for a moment. "I have to tell you, Brock, I have a better idea, but I'm not sure if it's the right decision."

Brock stared at his friend, but didn't speak.

After a moment, Walt continued, "A Seven Seas team is not far from here. They could probably be here by this evening."

"Well I don't see any problem with that, in fact it would work out perfect to get help from someone in the company. We could keep the situation in-house until we get Barb back safely."

"Yea, but the problem is, they're a family, a husband, a wife, and two young kids."

"Oh, I see. That's a tough call. Do you know them well?"

"No," Walt admitted. "I've only met them in person once. They seem like upstanding people, but it's a tough call when kids are involved."

"That's why you make the big money. It's your decision to make; I'm staying out of it. Whatever you decide, you know I'm with you."

"I know, Brock, and I appreciate it." He hesitated a second. "Give me your phone, I'm calling the Hathaways. Barb's in trouble and we're nowhere near any type of formal authority. We have to do something; we need help and that's it," Walt said in a determined tone.

Brock held out his phone, smiled and said, "Never had a

doubt. You always do the right thing. We'll just have to be extra careful where it concerns the kids."

Walt stared at the phone for a brief time. At last, he looked at Brock and said, "I don't have their number and I don't know it off hand."

16

_____

A t that instant the phone rang. The ring tone and vibrating phone startled Walt to the extent he dropped the phone in the sand. The tune from the Budweiser commercials grew progressively louder. He glanced at Brock for a second before reaching down and retrieving the phone. When Walt saw the name of the caller on the screen, a wide smile crossed his face.

Brock saw his expression and asked, "What is it?"

"It's not what it is," Walt said with a laugh, "it's who it is." He put the phone to his ear, pushed the talk button, and said, "Denny Smith, you old pirate. How are you?"

At the mention of Denny's name, Brock cocked his head and grinned.

Denny's reply came in his easy, laid back voice, "I'm good, Walt. How about yourself?"

"Good, good. How's Lynn?"

"She's fine," Denny said. "She's a healthy mother carrying a healthy baby." Almost as an afterthought, he added, "I called Brock. What are you doing with his phone?"

"Listen Denny, Brock is here with me and we're in a predicament."

"Somehow that doesn't surprise me."

"Barb's been kidnapped."

Even over the phone Walt could feel Denny's jovial mood change. His voice took on an urgent tone. "By who? Where is she?"

"We're not sure who took her or why, but we think we know where she is. The problem is . . . Brock and I are marooned on a deserted island. The Hathaways, a new family of Seven Seas field reporters, are in the vicinity and we need a boat. I don't have their number handy. Time is of the essence, Denny. Do you think you can get it for me?"

"Hang on," Denny said. Walt heard Denny speaking in a muffled voice before he came back on the phone. "Lynn is getting the number now."

"That's good news. Brock and I are going to try to get to the tiny atoll where we think they're holding her and liberate our boss."

"We're here so if there's more we can do, we'd be happy to lend a hand."

Walt held the phone at arm's length. For a long moment he stared in astonishment before returning the phone to his ear. "You're where?"

"Lynn and I are in Tahiti. We flew in today thinking we'd surprise everyone."

"Oh, you surprised us all right. Do you have a plane?"

"I rented a nifty little single engine craft, so yeah, whatever you need us to do."

"I'll give you the coordinates. You won't be able to land anywhere out here, but you could fly reconnaissance over the area. That would be a big help."

Brock had remained silent as he listened to Walt's end of

the conversation. Though he was quiet, his mind worked double-time. "We could also use a few things. Maybe Denny could drop some needed supplies while he's flying over."

"Good idea," Walt said. The two discussed what they needed most and relayed the list to Denny.

Denny agreed to get the items and fly over the island later that afternoon. When he ended the call, he looked at his wife and said, "We'll get the stuff Walt needs and get the plane ready, but you should stay here for this flight."

Lynn did not look impressed. "You know better than that. There's no way I'm staying here."

"Normally I wouldn't even suggest such a thing, but in your condition, you should stay here."

Shaking her head, Lynn said, "Not a chance."

"What if something happens and we have to ditch the plane? You're six months pregnant, you won't be able to swim."

"I'll just float on my big fat belly," Lynn said, smiling.

"Seriously, Lynn, this isn't just about you and me, we have the baby to think about."

"Oh no you don't. You're not going to put this on me. If you're going, I'm going. End of story."

Denny threw up his arms in frustration. He knew his wife and knew it was fruitless to continue arguing. Sometimes you win, sometimes you lose. End of story.

Mitchell Hathaway stood below deck at the onboard control panel. Along with his wife Claire, he always made it a point to show his children, Andrew and Brianna every aspect of sailing. Andrew, his son stood next to him and watched as Mitch described how to program the GPS. Due to the fact he was only twelve-years old, Andrew looked short standing next to his six-foot-four-inch father in the cabin of their fifty-foot sailboat.

"That's the basics," Mitch said. "We'll go over it again tomorrow."

"It's a lot to remember," Andrew said.

"Don't worry, after you've done it a few times it'll seem easy. I won't put something on you that you're not ready for. It doesn't matter how many times you have to do it before you get it, the main thing is getting it right."

Just then, Mitchell's satellite phone rang. He didn't have Brock's number and didn't recognize the number. However, the odds of receiving a mistake phone call out here in the middle of the Pacific had to be low so he pushed the talk button and said, "Hello."

"Hello, Mitch? It's Walter Ulrich."

"Walt, good to hear from you. I didn't recognize the number."

"Yea I'm on Brock McGowen's phone. He's here with me."

"I haven't had a chance to meet Brock yet. I'm looking forward to doing so soon."

Walt snorted. "You might get to meet him sooner than you think. Mitch,I have some important news for you. Barb Kendall's been kidnapped."

Almost five full seconds of silence passed before Mitch asked, "Where did this happen?"

"Right here on a small atoll on the leeward side of Tahiti."

More silence. Finally, Mitch spoke, "She's here?"

"Yes, she flew in for a vacation a few days after I met with you and your family."

"Hang on one second, Walt." Mitch covered the mouthpiece of his phone and turned to his son. "Why don't you go up on deck and tell your mother to come down here? We have an important phone call. You can keep an eye on your sister until we're finished.

"OK, I'll send mom down," the boy called over his shoulder, already climbing up the stairs two at a time.

"Sorry for the delay, Walt. So, you say Barb Kendall was kidnapped?"

"Yes, it's a long story but the basics are, we stumbled upon a lost Spanish treasure buried on a tiny atoll ..."

When Walt finished speaking, Claire Hathaway was standing next to her husband in front of the communication table in the cabin. Mitch put the phone on speaker mode, so she could hear what Walt said.

Walt continued, "Supposedly, there's some kind of curse on the atoll or the treasure or both. Anyway, it's been here for hundreds of years and the locals don't want it removed. We're not sure why they took Barb, but it has something to do with the treasure."

"Is there a ransom demand?"

"No, maybe kidnapping is the wrong word. They just took her."

"That's terrible. If there's any way we can help, just give the word."

"Actually, that's the reason I called," Walt said. "Where are you now?"

"We're only a few hours north-northeast of Tahiti."

"You're that close?"

Mitch replied, "Yes, the water is abundant with sea life and we were shooting some video of the region before sailing north."

"OK, here's the situation. Brock and I are on the atoll

where the treasure is buried. Denny and Lynn Smith are on the island of Tahiti."

"Denny and Lynn Smith are here too?"

"Yes, and they have access to a plane. The atoll where Barb is being held is within eyesight of where me and Brock are. The problem is, Denny can't land the plane and we can't get to Barb without a boat."

"We have a boat and we can be there soon," Claire said.

Recognizing her voice, Walt said, "I don't want to put your kids in danger, Claire. There must be some way of doing this without endangering your family."

Mitch and Claire exchanged knowing glances. Mitch spoke up, "There doesn't seem to be many alternatives. It's not like we can put them ashore somewhere and come back and pick them up."

Claire added, "I'd rather have them with us than stranded on a deserted island, mate," her Australian accent coming through.

"These people have tried to kill us. I've been shot with an arrow and Barb's been shot with a gun. We're both OK, but we were lucky."

"Still," Claire insisted, "I want my kids with me. No offense, Walt, but we're wasting time. If Barb needs us, we need to stop wanking around and get moving."

Mitch smiled at her comments. When it came to the people she was close to, his wife was a straight shooter, and he hoped Walt wouldn't be put off by her bold approach.

Neither Mitch nor Claire could see the broad smiles spreading across both Walt and Brock's faces.

"Fair enough. I'll give you the coordinates to our position. When you approach, try to look like you are just out for a cruise. Once we're on board your boat, we'll craft a plan to get Barb back."

"Sounds good," Mitch said. He took the coordinates down and ended the call. "Can you prepare to get us under-way," he asked Claire. "I'll be up in a minute."

As soon as she went up the stairs, he went to the state-room and worked the numbers on a combination lock on a large safe. When he swung the door open, the safe revealed a shotgun and a handgun. Mitch looked the firearms over, worked the actions on both, and replaced them in the safe. He hoped they wouldn't be needed, but his years in the Marine Corps would serve him well if they were.

17

Denny flew through a passing squall as he gained altitude and cleared the volcanic mountains of Tahiti. The squall was nothing more than a brief shower and within a quarter mile Denny flew back into bright sunshine. With Lynn occupying the passenger seat they set a course for Walt and Brock's location. The flight would only take ten minutes, so Lynn used the time to prepare for the drop.

She gathered everything Walt had asked for and stuffed it into a large mesh bag. Swim fins, snorkel gear, and dive knives along with dive lights and a hundred-foot length of rope went into the bag. Walt had no way of knowing what he would need in the hours ahead, therefore he tried to acquire things that could come in handy. Guns would have been his first choice, but he did not know where to look for them on the island.

Soon, the atolls came into view. Denny maintained a higher than normal altitude, so he could see the big picture as he flew, then he dropped to three-hundred feet. As they waited on the beach, Walt and Brock heard the plane coming from a good distance away. When it approached, they both strode out into the shallow water away from the thick foliage on the atoll. This gave the men far more visibility from the air.

"There they are," Lynn said.

Denny looked down and saw two men waving their arms. "I see them."

He tipped his wings to let them know he spotted them as he passed over. "I'm going to circle. Get ready to drop the sack when we pass over next time."

Denny swung out over the atoll before banking and heading back toward the men. Before he turned the plane, he saw the other speck of coral and sand. That had to be the atoll where Walt thought they were holding Barb. Denny took a quick glance at the atoll, then focused on flying slow and as close to Walt and Brock as he could get. He did not see the helicopter lifting off from the far side of the distant atoll.

When Denny brought the plane over the island for the second time, Lynn dropped the mesh bag close to where her friends stood. The bag drifted slightly and landed twenty feet away from Walt and Brock in about six-feet of clear water. Walt waded out to his waist, then swam closer. The bag lay in plain sight on the sea bed. Walt took a deep breath and dove to the bottom. He grabbed the bag and brought it to shore. Walt had just opened the drawstrings on the bag when he heard a loud bang. Both he and Brock looked skyward just in time to see dark smoke billowing from Denny's plane.

Denny hadn't seen the helicopter until it was too late. After Lynn had dropped the bag, he went into another slow bank. That's when he saw it. The helicopter flew straight in beside his wing and someone opened fire with an automatic rifle. The other aircraft flew in so close Denny could see the muzzle flashes as the gunman targeted his plane.

"Hang on!" he shouted.

With a quick kneejerk reaction, Denny banked the plane away at a sharp angle. He opened up the throttle and put distance between himself and the slower helicopter. The action came too late. Several slugs tore into the fuselage and ruptured an oil line. The engine immediately began to lose power.

"I'm going to try to get us away from the atoll," Denny told Lynn.

"The farther away we get, the harder it will be to swim back," Lynn said in a worried tone.

"I know, but if we put down close to the island, they'll just shoot us from the helicopter. If we can get far enough away, they might not know we're ditching."

Lynn looked back and saw the helicopter coming after them. "That's not working. They're following us."

Denny dropped farther and flew less than seventy-five feet above the surface of the ocean. A bullet found one of the rods connecting to the rudder and he struggled to control the aircraft. Having the helicopter come in from above would be fatal, but as he tried to gain altitude, the plane felt slow to respond. He'd only gained thirty feet and the helicopter was almost directly over the plane when Lynn noticed something on the water.

"Look," she said, pointing, "There's a boat sailing this way."

Denny saw it and immediately halted his attempt to gain altitude. "I'm going to try to land this thing as close to that boat as I can get. It's going to be a bumpy landing so hold on tight. As soon as we stop moving, get out. Don't hesitate, don't wonder what I'm doing, just get out right away. The plane will sink fast, you have to move even faster, understand?"

Lynn took a deep breath. "I understand."

"When you get out, swim for that sailboat. The helicopter might not go after them for fear of getting too many civilians involved. Sooner or later, there will have to be an investigation and there is only so much anyone can cover up."

"It looks like the helicopter is backing off already," Lynn said.

"Yep, that's good," he replied. "Now all we have to do is survive a plane crash and get rescued by strangers and we'll be OK."

He slowed the air speed more until the plane almost hovered at its lowest flying speed. Any slower and the engine would stall. Denny dropped until the plane was almost skimming the blue sea. They were approaching the pleasure boat. Denny wanted to time it right so the plane came down just to the side of the boat. Finally, he killed the engine altogether.

The eerie sound of the rushing wind gave Lynn a feeling of pure terror.

The wheels hit the water first and almost sent the nose diving under the surface. That would have been disastrous, but Denny held the yoke back and kept the nose elevated and just above water. The plane bounced before coming down again. This time it sank all the way to the underside of the fuselage. After taking two short skips, the light craft settled on the surface and came to an abrupt stop.

Lynn heralded her husband's advice. Moving as fast as her six-month pregnant belly would allow, she undid her harness, stood, and pushed herself through the open window. Lynn hit the water and sank a good distance below the surface before she began to swim to the top. When she surfaced, she didn't see Denny. She stroked hard and swam away from the aircraft, as it yielded to the weight of the water. Seawater poured in, filling the cockpit, and sinking the plane.

A sound from behind caught her attention. Lynn swung around in time to swallow a mouthful of seawater from the bow wave of the sail boat which was passing close by. An orange life preserver floated through the air and landed three feet away. Lynn paddled to the flotation device and gripped it tight. A rope was tied to the life preserver and she hung on as she was pulled to the hull of the sail boat. Long, solid arms reached over the side and she was hoisted onto the deck of the boat by a tall man.

Without speaking, the man took the life ring from Lynn's hands, wound up and gave it a mighty throw. Lynn's gaze followed the ring and watched it land within five feet of Denny, who was treading water not far away. It took a second, but then Lynn realized he was injured. When Denny tried to swim, he favored one side.

"He's hurt," she said to the tall man who held the other end of the rope beside her on the deck.

Mitch Hathaway handed Lynn the rope and said, "Pull us in when we get to the flotation device."

Lynn noticed a small boy and even smaller girl manning the sails. "Take in that headsail," he told them. To a woman standing at the helm he said, "Keep her steady now."

With that, he took two strides to the starboard rail and dove into the blue South Pacific water. He was halfway to Denny before his head broke the water. Mitch held onto Denny with one arm while he stroked with the other.

"OK, pull us in!" he yelled to Lynn.

As the sail boat was passing the men in the water, she

frantically pulled the rope. In another few seconds the boat would pass the men. Lynn worked hard pulling the rope hand over hand. Then, the boat slowed drastically. The children had furled the sails.

With Mitch Hathaway stroking and kicking and Lynn pulling on the rope, the men came up to the hull of the boat.

"Give us some slack," Mitch said to Lynn. "We'll swing around to the stern and climb up the ladder."

Lynn played out some slack until the men were at the stern. Claire Hathaway left her position at the helm and rushed to the aid of her husband. With their combined effort, they hauled Denny out of the water. As Lynn hurried to his side, she could see the unnatural angle of his foot.

Lynn spoke in a worrisome tone, "Denny are you alright?"

Denny coughed a bit, then said, "I've had better days. That was a hard landing." He looked at Mitch and Claire and added, "I guess I shouldn't complain. Things could have been much worse if you guys hadn't come along. My wife and I owe you our lives."

"Glad to be of assistance. And you don't owe us a thing, it was nothing more than anyone would have done," Mitch said.

In her Australian cadence Claire added, "That's right. We're just glad we made it in time. Walt said these wankers are dangerous. We didn't see exactly what happened, but we did see that helicopter chasing you."

"Did you say Walt?" asked Lynn.

"Sure thing mate. You are Denny and Lynn Smith, aren't you?"

"Yes."

"We're the Hathaways," Mitch announced. "Walt asked us to assist. He told us you were here."

At six-foot-four, his lanky frame appeared almost too large for an oceangoing sail boat. A friend of the late Art Kendall, Mitch had jumped at the chance to sail the seas while reporting on various ocean activities.

He had met Art in the Marine Corps. When Mitch got out and returned to his home state of California, he kept in close contact with Art.

Clair hailed from Australia. She had started racing sail boats at the early age of ten and handled their boat with confidence. Claire almost matched her husband in height and like her husband, she too had a lanky frame.

Lynn smiled, stuck out her hand and said, "Nice to meet you."

Claire shook her hand first. "Nice to meet you too. We've heard a great deal about you and it's good to put faces to the names. Now, if you'll excuse me, I have to look after my kids and steer the boat. We'll catch up later." With that, Claire headed toward the helm giving orders to the children as she went.

The Hathaways were on assignment from Seven Seas documenting life on and around South Pacific coral reefs. The assignment was a true family affair. Along with Mitch and Claire were their twelve-year old son Andrew, their eight-year old daughter Brianna, and their friendly four-year-old Australian Sheepdog, Shooter.

Mitch placed the life preserver under Denny's head. "Do you have pain anywhere else?" he asked.

"I think I hit my head. I feel woozy and I might be sick."

Turning his attention to Lynn, Mitch said, "Keep an eye on him and try to make him comfortable. I'm going for the first aid kit, I'll be right back."

Mitch directed the activity on the deck of the *Sea Spray*. He wanted to administer first aid and get the situation under control, so he told the children to furl the sails and let the boat drift for the time being. Next, he talked to Claire for a moment. She assured her husband she'd keep a sharp eye on the kids and their surroundings. She would be on the lookout for unwanted surprises.

When he felt certain the situation was under control above deck, Mitch went below. First, he retrieved the first aid kit from an overhead cabinet. Next, he worked the combination lock on the steel locker mounted to the wall. Mitch took out a shotgun and a semiautomatic handgun and two boxes of shells for each.

18

From where they sat on the beach, Walt and Brock could not see what had happened to Denny's plane. They merely saw the helicopter firing at it and the plane flying out of sight, trailing a cloud of black smoke. After the helicopter fired on the plane, it swerved down, and the gunman opened fire on Walt and Brock. The action came too late for they were already moving into the thick brushy cover. The shots went wild. After only one volley, the helicopter flew away.

"Come on, let's see what's going on," Walt said, jumping up and urging Brock to follow. The two men sprinted toward the opposite side of the island hoping to get a better view of what happened to Denny's plane.

When they got to the far side, Walt looked up and saw the helicopter landing on the atoll. He scanned the sky, but the brush hindered his line of sight. With Brock a step behind, he followed the trail to the spot where he'd confronted the men the previous day. Stepping right up to the edge of the water, Walt gazed out to sea. Denny's plane was nowhere in sight.

"Damn, he must have gone down," Brock lamented.

Walt continued to scan the horizon. Finally, he saw an object out on the water. "There," he said pointing. "There's something out there." After a moment, he said, "I can make out sails. It's a sailboat."

"Yes, you're right, it is a sailboat."

"I wonder if that's Mitch."

"I don't know, but whoever it is must have seen what happened to Denny and Lynn. We need to talk to them."

Walt nodded in agreement. "I'd bet money it's Mitch, but if not . . . we need to figure out how to get that boat over here."

"Do you have matches or a lighter or anything to get a fire started?"

"No, nothing. I should have had Denny bring something, but it slipped my mind."

Brock sighed. "I guess I'll have to resort back to my Boy Scout training and start a fire by rubbing stones together."

Walt frowned. He thought his old friend was joking. Twenty minutes later, a smoky fire burned along the shore of the island.

Sixty yards from shore, Mitch gave the order and his son Andrew Hathaway released the lever that dropped the anchor over the side. The anchor line sang as it played out. The sail boat swung on the current until she lay moored parallel to the atoll. Even from that distance Mitch recognized one of the men waving his arms on the beach.

"Look, it's Walt, and that must be Brock," he said to Claire as he waved back.

Claire waved. Then she heard the satellite phone ringing. "Hello. This is Claire Hathaway."

"It's Walt. Good to see you."

"You too, Walt. We'll send the inflatable raft over as soon as we can get it unloaded."

"Hang on, Claire." Walt turned to Brock and asked, "Are you up for a swim? We can swim out there and be on the boat long before they can get a raft to us."

"Sure, let's do it."

Speaking into the phone again, Walt said, "Don't bother with the raft, Claire, we'll swim out."

With that, he ended the call and began to put his swim fins on. Brock covered the small fire with sand before donning his own fins. When they were set, the men waded into the water and began to swim out to the boat. Once they cleared the reef, they had easy swimming in the dead calm, warm ocean.

When they approached, Mitch called out, "Come around to the starboard side. There's a ladder at the stern."

Walt and Brock followed his instructions and less than a minute later they were climbing the ladder to the deck of the *Sea Spray*. That's when Walt noticed Lynn and Denny on the deck. She sat with her back against the gunwale cradling Denny's head in her hands.

Walt stood and stared in stunned silence.

Brock blurted out, "Holy smokes, I didn't expect to see you guys here!"

Denny smiled but he looked weak.

Lynn said, "A helicopter shot us down. We had to ditch in the ocean."

Mitch, Claire, and their kids were already busy pulling anchor and setting sails.

"I think we should keep moving," Mitch called from the

stern where he quickly wrapped up the rope connected to the life preserver. "If one of you will lend a hand, I'll have Claire show you the way to the stateroom. You can take Denny down and get him set up there. He'll be a lot more comfortable that way."

Walt spoke up. "Good idea. I'll help out above deck. Brock, you can help get Denny squared away."

Brock gave Walt a salute. "Aye aye, sir." Then he knelt beside his old friend. "So, this is how you take your wife on vacation. I would think you'd have more sense than that Mr. Smith. You know she's expecting, right?"

Denny laughed through gritted teeth. "You're always good for a laugh, you old pirate."

Brock turned his attention to Lynn, "What are his injuries?"

"He's got a broken ankle for sure and probably a concussion," she replied. "He's got a few other bumps and bruises, but that's the worst. His ankle is really bad. He'll probably need surgery."

"Well, it's always good to see the two of you no matter the circumstances. Let's get him below where he can be pampered."

While the others were busy with Denny, Walt gave Mitch a hand. He took the helm until the sails were set, then handed over the wheel to the captain, Mitch. The kids worked the deck, helping make the boat ready for sailing. Walt could tell they were experienced sailors. With the jobs done, Andrew and his little sister Brianna joined Walt and their father at the helm.

"Is that man going to be alright, Daddy?" Brianna asked.

"He's got at least one broken bone," Mitch answered looking at Walt. "It's a serious injury and he'll need medical care real soon, but he should come out of it OK."

Gazing at the sky, Andrew asked, "Do you think the helicopter will come back?"

Mitch did not water things down for his children. "That's hard to say, but that's the reason why I wanted to get under way as quickly as we could. They might be looking for Walt and his friend Brock. We don't want to hang around and wait for them to come back. We want to look like we're nothing more than tourists out for a day sail."

Walt said, "Maybe you should take us in. There's no need to place your kids in danger. We can find another way."

"And leave Barb out there?" Mitch spun the wheel turning the boat and heading away from the atoll and the treasure, "Besides, my kids like danger, isn't that right, Bri?" He grabbed his daughter by the waist and tickled her. The eight-year old loved it. She giggled and squirmed and scolded her father until he let go of her.

"I just don't want anyone else to get hurt. Denny and Lynn came to help and look what happened. It seems like every time I'm in a fix and someone shows up to help, something bad happens to them. Two nights ago, a man snuck aboard Brock's boat with a knife. His boat ended up getting stolen."

"I hear you, Walt, and believe me I'm not reckless with my children. They're my entire world. I do believe in involving my kids in activities outside of school. Life lessons aren't learned in the classroom, they're learned through living." After a moment of silence, he added, "Besides, we must do all we can for Barb, right?"

Walt's emotions caught up to him and a nod was all he could muster. Once again, he found himself among men and women who were a cut above the average. People who you could count on and who would stick with you through thick and thin. Barb Kendall was the love of his life. Brock McGowen and Denny and Lynn Smith were his best friends. Now Mitch and Claire Hathaway were also stepping up to the plate to help. He knew he had the best help the world could offer.

With sails full, the agile sailing vessel made way over gentle swells. Mitch set a course to the south-southwest, away from the cluster of coral atolls. They needed to be out of sight and mind while they made plans for the next phase of their adventure. Thunder rolled in the distance as dark clouds signaled a squall on the horizon.

"Dad, look!" Andrew called. He stood at the stern and pointed back toward the atolls.

"That didn't take long," Mitch said, when he saw the boat speeding toward them. In the next instant, the helicopter rose from the atoll, and it too started in their direction.

"That's what I was afraid of," Walt remarked. "The men in the helicopter probably saw you pluck Denny and Lynn from the ocean. They won't want word of this to get back to the main island, so they'll come after you. It doesn't matter if they think you're tourists or Barb's friends out to rescue her. They want to silence you."

Mitch only took a second to respond. "Bri honey, go bring your mother up here." He glanced at his pursuers and appraised the situation. The helicopter wasn't making an effort to come close to the *Sea Spray*. "The chopper's waiting for the speedboat. They'll come at us together, probably with the chopper laying down suppressing fire and the men in the boat boarding us."

"Sounds like you know your tactics."

"I spent six years in the Marine Corps. Recon. Anyway, that's how I would do it."

Claire Hathaway reached the deck and asked, "What's going on?"

Mitch gestured toward the stern. "We're about to have company and they're not friendly."

"Crikey. I'm getting sick of these wankers messing with us. I think it's about time we give them something to worry about."

Mitch handed the wheel over to his wife and said, "Exactly what I was thinking. I'll be right back."

"All right then kids, downstairs you go. You'll be safer below deck," Claire said.

The children followed their father down the stairs.

Walt watched as the speedboat came on strong. "That boat is going to catch us very soon."

Claire stared ahead. With a lift of her chin she gestured toward the horizon where dark blue, almost black storm clouds were gathering. "We're all going to have something else to worry about in about ten minutes."

Walt wondered how she could predict the time the storm would hit, but he remembered Claire Hathaway had been an expert sailor for many years before she met Mitchell and settled down to raise a family. The athletic Aussie competed in sailing events all over the world and even won a Bronze Medal in the Olympic Games.

"So, if we can hold them off for ten minutes, we might have a better chance," Walt said.

"Yes . . . well it's hard to say what might happen in a storm. It would cancel out some of their advantages anyway."

Mitch came up on deck looking like John Rambo. He wore a sheath knife on his belt and had another strapped to his calf. In one hand he carried the shotgun. In the other he had an aluminum baseball bat. The handgun was stuffed into his waistband. He strode up to Walt and familiarized him with the weapons.

"Twelve-gauge pump-action shotgun," Mitch said, laying the gun on the deck. He produced a box of shells and placed them on the deck beside the gun. He also laid the bat next to the gun. Removing the handgun from his waistband, he said, "Nine-millimeter Browning. Holds nine shots, eight in the clip, and one in the chamber. Here's an extra loaded clip."

Walt said, "These weapons give us a chance, but a close-range gunfight is a good way to get some of us shot."

"I agree. We either have to try to take them by surprise and take out as many as we can right away, or play it cool and not bring out the weapons unless it's a last resort."

Walt spent a few seconds thinking. At last he said, "The thing that worries me is that helicopter. We might be able to take the men in the boat by surprise, but the helicopter will shoot the hell out of us if we do."

"Yea, you're right. Allowing the men in the boat to board us could work. We'd have to come up with a way to lure the chopper close enough to take it out. One thing that's not going to happen though," Mitch declared with certainty, "is I am not going to be taken prisoner. I'm not giving up control of my life and family to whoever these bastards are. If it comes to it, I'm fighting, whether I have to use a baseball bat, knife, or my hands."

"Fair enough. Let's hope it doesn't come to that."

19

Barb heard the thunder in the distance. She also heard the rotors as the helicopter took off again. This was the second time she'd heard it leave. Something important must be going on she reasoned. The brightness of the light seeping into the hut through the cracks had diminished greatly and Barb knew a storm would hit very soon. She decided to make a move now while her captors were hopefully preoccupied by the storm.

Barb had not been able to untie her hands, but she worked them down to the base of the pole she'd been fastened to. By digging her hands deep into the sandy soil, she was able to slide the knot under the bottom end of the pole. Although her hands were tied behind her back, Barb was no longer attached to the pole. Now she had to find something to cut her hands free. Searching the sparse hut, Barb came up empty.

Her next move would have to be escape. She sneaked to the door of the hut and peeked out through a crack. One man sat by a fire ring reading a magazine. The man wore traditional garb the same as her, but he was bare chest with a crown of leaves around his head and a grass skirt, he looked out of place wearing heavy rimmed glasses and reading a Motor Trend magazine.

The man sat directly in front of the hut and there was no way out without him seeing her. Barb scoured the hut where the poles met the sand, but she couldn't find an opening to squeeze out through. She would have to take on the guard. She thought for a minute and came up with a plan. A coconut bowl was the only loose object in the hut. Barb ignored the bowl since she could not swing it with her hands tied behind her back. She went back to the center of the hut and sat against the pole once again.

When she was ready, she started calling out just loud enough for the man to hear, "Hey. Hey out there, I need to use the washroom. Hey out there!"

Barb kept up the talk until finally the man poked his head through the door. "What is wrong?" he asked.

"I need to use the washroom."

"There is no washroom here," he stated, ducking his head, and entering the small hut.

"I can go behind some bushes or something. I don't care where, I need to go," Barb said with urgency in her voice.

A malevolent grin creased the guard's face. "Maybe I should watch, just to keep an eye on you."

Barb ignored the insidious statement. She said, "Cut me loose, and hurry."

When the guard bent down to unfasten her wrists, she brought her knees up into his head as hard as she could in a scissors motion. Her knees connected with his head with a thump. The guard staggered in his crouched position before falling backward and landing sprawled out on the sand floor. Barb didn't waste time and showed no pity for her captor. She jumped on the man and repeatedly drove knee after knee into his midsection and face.

Despite her best intentions, this only worked to infuriate the man and cause him to focus. With one hand, he stopped a knee aimed at his groin. He used the other hand to clamp onto Barb's throat. The viselike hand squeezed the energy out of her kicks and she quickly lost the urge to fight. Now, Barb struggled to survive. With her hands tied behind her back, she felt defenseless. The guard squeezed tighter and Barb felt the energy draining from her body. Another two seconds and the world began to go dark.

She allowed her limp body to slide off to the side. This caused the guard to release his grip. Barb gasped for air. She felt as if she was breathing through a plastic bag. The guard stood over her and raised a clenched fist. Fighting through the fog in her mind, Barb felt certain the blow would break bones in her face. At the last second, the guard seemed to get a hold of himself. He halted the punch and gave her a playful slap on the cheek instead.

"It would be a shame to damage such a beautiful creature as you," he said in an adoring tone. "Especially before we get to offer you to our god."

Barb's strength slowly returned. Her breathing steadied and her vision cleared. The guard's last statement hit home. So that's why they were keeping her alive . . . to sacrifice her to some make-believe God. In this day and age, it seemed a senseless way to go.

She said, "What a waste. You think your life will be better because you murdered me?"

"It is not murder my pretty little thing. Blank rewards true believers and punishes those who are not. Few true believers are left in today's society. This act of sacrifice will go a long way in procuring our place in the heavens.

"No, your life will not change for the better. You'll have a murder on your hands. Most likely you'll be caught within days and spend the rest of your life inside a prison."

"We will not be caught."

"People will be looking for me," Barb insisted. "Even if they don't catch you right away, they won't stop until they find the truth. That's how your life is going to change. You will be looking over your shoulder for the rest of your life, or until you are caught."

The guard slapped her face for real this time. "I have heard enough of your evil talk. You will serve your purpose tonight."

Barb caught the coppery taste of blood in her mouth. Her face stung from the hard slap and her ears rang. She didn't want to risk another blow, but she thought her words were getting through to the man.

"You know I'm right. You're throwing away my life, your life, and the lives of everyone else who's involved.

A spark of hate flickered in the guard's eye for a second, but it soon dissipated. He smiled and stood, pulling Barb to her feet. "You are very brave to talk the way you do in the face of danger. We will see how brave you talk tonight when the fire licks at your feet."

He forced her to sit against the pole again. This time he tied not only her hands to the pole, but her arms were also fastened. Before he left, the guard bound Barb's feet together leaving her totally helpless. Her physical condition matched her mental state for she also felt totally helpless.

20

M itch sailed as close to the wind as he could and headed for the oncoming storm. The chasing boat steadily closed the distance while the helicopter chose to stay back, hovering closer to the atoll. Walt took up a position behind the mast with the shotgun in hand. He loaded the 870 Remington Wingmaster with five shotgun shells filled with one and a half drams of smokeless powder and number seven and a half shot. That particular-sized shot would spread out in a two- to four-foot pattern at twenty yards and be very effective at close range. The problem was, getting the target in close range.

Mitch spotted three men in the boat. Two held rifles and pointed them in his general direction. The third man operated the outboard tiller and brought the smaller, faster speedboat alongside the *Sea Spray*.

"Stop. You are going to be boarded," said the man in the bow of the boat.

Mitch heard the helicopter approaching. He cupped his hands over his mouth and called, "Who are you?"

"Stop now. We are coming aboard."

Mitch nodded to Claire, who was now on deck. She nodded back and began to throw a luff in the main sail. The *Sea Spray* slowed, and Claire secured a line from the speedboat to a cleat on the larger sail boat. The first man climbed aboard, then held his hand out for the second man.

Mitch looked at Walt. Keeping his voice slightly above a whisper, he said, "I can't do it. I'm not going to allow these thugs aboard my boat while my kids are here."

Walt simply said, "It's time for plan B." He came to his feet and brought the shotgun up with the agility of a cat. With the gun shouldered, he crept toward the starboard side where Claire stood next to the intruder.

Mitch pulled the handgun from where he had it tucked into his waistband at the small of his back. He was a man who spent a lot of time, and who felt at home on a boat rocking on an unstable sea. With confident, steady steps, he approached the man.

Claire saw him coming. The man was leaning over the rail holding his hand out to assist the second man up. She tapped him on the shoulder and said, "Excuse me."

When the man turned around, he noticed Mitch coming at him with the handgun in shooting position. The man's eyes grew wide. Forgetting about his friend who was still in the speedboat, the man spun and began to raise his rifle. Mitch fired two quick shots into the man's chest. He staggered sideways, hovered for a second, and crumpled to the deck.

Walt sprang into action. He made it to the rail before Mitch. Pointing the barrel of the gun toward the men in the boat, he shouted, "Hands up!"

The man in the middle of the boat already had his rifle halfway to his shoulder. He fired off a reckless shot that snapped off into the clouds. Walt pulled the trigger and felt the gun kick as the pellets sprayed the boat. He pulled back as soon as he shot. A moan came from the boat, but another rifle shot flew overhead. Walt crouched and moved toward the bow of the sailboat. He heard the speedboat's motor cough to life.

"We can't let them get away!" he yelled to Mitch.

Mitch snapped off three quick shots over the side, but he didn't want to risk leaning over the side. Therefore, he couldn't see if he'd hit anyone.

Walt said, "Give me some more covering fire."

Mitch obliged and sent another five-round volley down toward the speedboat. When Walt ventured a look over the side, the man at the tiller had already begun to pull the boat away from the hull of the *Sea Spray*. Staring down the bead of the shotgun, Walt aimed at the man and pulled the trigger. He worked the pump ejecting the spent shell and loading a fresh one into the chamber. Walt swung the scattergun toward the other man in the boat and pulled the trigger again. He saw the man slump forward. Mitch popped a fresh clip into his nine-millimeter and trained it on the men in the boat. The extra bullets weren't needed. The men in the boat didn't move. The shotgun had done the job.

The helicopter bore down on the drifting *Sea Spray*. Claire kicked the rifle away from the man lying in a pool of his own blood. She leaned over the rifle and found its safety catch. The safety was off. Claire remained bent over as the helicopter flew low directly over the boat. With wind from the rotor threatening to knock her off her feet, Claire stood, shouldered the rifle, and began to fire. Her first target was the man sitting in the open doorway aiming an automatic rifle at her husband. She pulled the trigger in quick succession firing six shots. Three bullets slammed into the man. Two bullets tore into his midsection, one barreled through his leg. He dropped his rifle as he was driven backward into the helicopter.

Next, she focused on the pilot. Claire stood with her legs at shoulder width apart and emptied the rifle's magazine. A myriad of holes blossomed in the windshield as several of the slugs found their target. The helicopter started to spin. For a frightening moment, Claire thought it might come down right on top of the boat. However, after two full revolutions, the helicopter spun away. Less than ten seconds after she'd fired, the bird hit the surface of the sea with a crash. A fiery explosion erupted and everyone on thedeck of the *Sea Spray* could feel the heat as a rush of air passed over the deck.

Brock had been waiting, out of sight on the stairs leading to the cabin with the baseball bat at the ready. When he heard the explosion, he hustled to the deck and joined the others along the starboard rail. As they looked on, the motor sputtered and died leaving the speedboat drifting haplessly on the mounting waves. The man at the tiller appeared to be moving.

Wind whipped through the *Sea Spray*'s rigging and the boat began to pitch as it rode the swells.

Mitch looked at Claire with a broad grin. "I don't think the *Sea Spray* has even got a scratch on her. That was good thinking and good shooting."

Claire blushed. With shaky hands she lay the rifle down. "I'm just glad the threat is over. I'm going to check on the kids."

"Good idea. We need to get these sails down or we'll lose them."

"I'll bring Andrew up. I'm leaving Bri below. She's too small to help much and it's too dangerous in this wind and sea," Claire said, heading for the cabin.

Before the others left the rail, Brock pointed and said, "Look, he's standing up."

Against all odds, the man at the tiller of the speedboat was still alive. He stood on wobbly legs and began to move around in the boat.

"What's he doing?" Mitch wondered.

Walt replied, "It doesn't look as though he knows what he's doing."

The man could not stand steady in the rocking boat. A violent three-foot wave hit the twenty-foot boat broadside and dumped the man over the side.

"He's in the water!" Brock exclaimed.

Mitch said, "We should go and get him. Even though he tried to kill us, it's the law of the sea and, he might be able to tell us what in God's name is going on."

The three men hurried to unfasten the inflatable dingy. They brought it to the rail and were about to pull the cord to initiate the self-inflating device, when Brock shouted, "Look, he's in trouble!"

Walt stopped what he was doing and stared at the scene unfolding one-hundred yards off the starboard rail. The man who had fallen into the ocean struggled to hang onto the speedboat. He could not see because his back was turned, but a large fin knifed through the choppy water directly toward where he clung to the boat.

First Walt, then Brock joined in yelling, "Hey! Behind you, there's a shark!"

Mitch retrieved the rifle Claire had used to bring down the helicopter, but he found the magazine empty. It didn't matter. The shark put on a burst of speed and made it to the man before anyone could do anything to save him. They watched as the twelve-foot long, grey-skinned animal swam right into the man. He was towed for a few feet before being pulled under. In a second, his head broke the surface and he gasped for air. Soon, the shark rose close to the surface again. Even from one-hundred yards Walt could discern what type of shark it was. The grey stripes and square head gave its breed away as a Tiger Shark. The shark made a half circle before moving in again. This time when the man went under, he never resurfaced.

Walt, Brock, and Mitch went back to work without speaking a word.

Claire and Andrew joined the men on deck. Lynn came up and handled the helm. She had been a charter Captain all her life and she piloted the boat with an expert hand. For the next hour the crew of the *Sea Spray* worked to keep her bow pointed into the wind and waves as she rode out the storm.

Over the roar of the wind, Walt called to Mitch, "We should try to make it to the atoll now, in the midst of the storm."

"You mean use the storm for cover?"

"Exactly. They'll never expect that."

Mitch hung onto the main mast as he thought about the proposition for a moment. The wind thrashed his face and rain mixed with salt water poured down on his head. Finally, he said, "You have a good idea if we can control the boat. That won't be an easy task in this storm though."

"It's your call. If you don't want to risk it, I'll understand."

"How would you get on the atoll? I'm not going to be able to drop you off right on the beach."

Walt stood next to Mitch at the mast. "I don't know for sure," he said. "Brock will go with me. We'll have to wing it when we get to that point."

A grin formed on Mitch's face. "You don't want to ask him first?"

"No. He'll go,"

Mitch continued prodding. "You like to wing it, don't you?"

"You know what they say."

"What's that?"

"If we don't live an adventurous life while we're young, we'll have to lie when we're old."

Mitch laughed. "I never heard that one, but I must say I like it." He stared back toward the atoll. "I'll tell you what, if you can find a way onto the atoll, I can get you close."

Walt brought Brock onto the deck. Although the rain had slowed slightly, the wind blew salt water over the deck drenching everyone as they clung to handholds at the mast and along the rails.

Walt started the conversation off. "Mitch and Claire are going to take the *Sea Spray* in close to the atoll where we think they're holding Barb. We have to figure out how to get on and off the atoll without being spotted."

"It's far too rough to use the inflatable," Brock noted.

"How close do you think you can get," Walt asked Mitch.

"That's hard to say. I don't know the depth of the water over the reef. Unless we can find a channel, I think it's fair to say we'll have to stay on the outside of the reef."

Walt said, "If we have to stay outside the reef, we'll need to use the inflatable."

"I have a small five horsepower motor for it."

Brock said, "Well, that changes everything. We should be able to get over the reef and into the shallows using a motor."

"That's it then," Walt said. "Mitch, you get us in as close as you can, and we'll use the inflatable to reach the atoll.

We'll take Brock's phone along. Just stay offshore and we'll give you a call when we're ready to come back aboard."

"It's settled then. I'm going to get the motor ready," Mitch said, heading for the forward compartment.

Brock gazed at Walt with a questioning look. "What are we going to do once we make landfall? How do we get Barb when we don't even know if she's there?"

"We'll have to play it as it unfolds. Whether she's there or not, someone knows where she is and I'm not leaving until I find her."

21

F orty minutes later the *Sea Spray* rode the storm toward
the small atoll like a ghost ship materializing out of
the dark grey horizon. Claire took Lynn's place at the helm
and expertly maneuvered the boat to within seventy-five
yards of the atoll's sandy shores. Unlike the other two atolls
Walt had visited, this one had a white sand beach ringing
the entire island. The atoll itself wasn't more than a narrow
strip of coral, sand, and low foliage protruding from the
South Pacific Ocean.

Mitch assisted in lowering the inflatable raft over the
starboard side where it wouldn't be seen from land. Walt
climbed over the railing and shimmied down the rope.
When he was standing in the raft on the roiling sea, he
shouted, "We'll see you soon, Mitch. Have a safe sail!"

Brock followed, albeit a little slower, and the two men
took up their respective positions in the raft. Walt sat in the
bow and Brock sat in the stern by the outboard motor. He
pulled the cable and the small motor kicked to life. A little
blue smoke, a sputter, and the motor settled to an even purr.

Mitch clung to the rail and watched the small raft

struggle through the five-foot waves. When the raft rounded the stern of the boat and headed toward the beach, he made his way aft to where Claire stood at the helm.

Claire raised her voice over the wind, "I'll say one thing, Walter Ulrich is indefatigable."

Mitch gazed at the tiny atoll. "Yes, he is. I hope he can find Barb."

Pulling hard on the wheel and turning the boat out to sea, Claire said, "We gave them the best chance to make it to the atoll unnoticed. Now we'll ride the storm out until they call, and when they do we'll give them the best chance we can get to make it back unscathed."

Mitch slid an arm around her waist and smiled. "I'm glad you're on our side."

Huge fountains of spray showered the men in the inflatable as they dodged over the roiling surface of the sea. Keeping the motor wide open, Brock turned toward land and rode a wave halfway in. The waves were breaking right on the narrow beach and they rode another wave right up onto the beach. Walt grabbed the shotgun and jumped out from the bow before the raft stopped moving. Brock wasn't far behind. They dragged the raft into the thick brush.

Walt watched the *Sea Spray* making way against the storm. The white hull and sails provided a stark contrast to the dark, broody sky. He spoke in a low tone. "Let's follow the line of the beach and see if we come across anything."

"Lead the way, pal," Brock said, gesturing toward the beach.

Staying alert and walking hunched over, the men snuck along the edge of the sand looking for footprints or anything else that stood out. They'd gone about a quarter of the way around the atoll when they came across a trail. The rain and wind had washed away any recent signs of human activity, but the trail was wide enough for foot traffic.

Walt led the way along the trail with Brock following a step behind. The storm began to ease as they came to the edge of a small clearing. Three hand-built huts with thatched roofs formed a semicircle with a fire pit in the center. No one was visible outside the huts.

Staying just outside the clearing, Walt said, "I don't see anyone, but we should inspect those huts."

Brock took the nine-millimeter from his waistband and replied, "Ready when you are."

The men silently covered the distance to the closest hut. With Brock pointing the gun at the door for cover, Walt opened the door and looked inside. The hut was empty. They moved to the second hut. Just as they reached the door a man came out. The man wore traditional garb . . . cloth loincloth, anklets, and bracelets made of local material, and a headdress constructed of local fronds. Walt didn't hesitate. He slammed the butt of the shotgun into the side of the man's head. The man dropped like a pile of bricks. Brock held the pistol on the unconscious man while Walt peered inside the entrance. This hut was also empty.

Voices could be heard coming from the third hut. Walt and Brock took up positions at the door. They exchanged knowing glances, then Walt slammed the door open and rushed inside. Three men sat in a circle in the room. Barb sat in the center tied to a pole.

"Freeze!" Walt yelled, keeping the shotgun leveled in front of him. "Anyone moves and they're dead."

Brock slipped in behind and kept the handgun trained on the men. "Line up along the wall. Now!"

The men looked shocked at the sudden intrusion. They obeyed and faced the wall on their knees. Walt crouched down and began to cut through the ropes binding Barb.

Barb wore an equally shocked expression. When she was free she threw her arms around his shoulders and said, "I thought you were dead."

Walt whispered in her ear. "I'm alive and I'm here. Let's go, we're getting you out of here."

Barb pulled away, squinted her eyes, and asked, "Brock, what are you doing here?"

"You know how you always get shot every time you go somewhere," Brock said in his comical, dry tone. "Well, I figured I'd better come out here and see if you need a hand."

Barb smiled. "I know there's more to the story, but for now, I'm glad you're here." Lifting onto her tip toes, she planted a light kiss on his cheek.

Walt said, "Let's have a nice reunion later. Right now, we need to wrap things up here and get off this tiny atoll."

They used lengths of rope found in the hut to tie the hands of the men facing the wall. When all three men were bound, they exited the hut.

"Uh oh," Brock said, pointing to the other hut. "Looks like our friend had better things to do."

The man that Walt had hit was gone. "Never mind. We'll just have to keep an eye out for him. Let's get to the beach and call Mitch."

"Mitch?" asked Barb.

Walt said, "Mitch Hathaway. It's a long story and it's one for another time. Let's go. After everything that has happened the last few days, we can't get away from these atolls quick enough."

Walt led the way and they almost reached the trail at the edge of the clearing, when the group found themselves surrounded. Six armed men stepped out from the brush forming a circle. Unlike the others in the huts, these men wore regular, modern clothes. They carried automatic rifles and had them pointed at Walt and his group. One man, who only carried a pistol, stepped forward and spoke, "Drop your weapons please."

Not wanting to be taken prisoner, Walt hesitated for a long moment but in the end, he laid the shotgun in the sand. Mitch still had the *Sea Spray* waiting offshore. That was their one ace in the hole. Although Denny was laid up, Mitch, Claire, and Lynn would make a formidable team. If Walt could keep everyone alive long enough, maybe help would be on the way.

"You," Brock hissed as he dropped his handgun to the sandy ground. He recognized the man as the front desk clerk at the hotel.

"Ah, hello, Mr. McGowen. I see you found what you were looking for."

"You set me up."

"No, I merely gave you the information you sought." The clerk took out a cigarette and lit it. "Thanks again for the smokes."

One of the men gathered up the weapons while another man went into the hut and came out with the men who were tied. He undid their bindings and they joined the other men surrounding Walt, Brock, and Barb. Walt noticed that all the men, no matter how they were dressed, had the same scroll and spear tattoos on their necks.

The clerk made a show of looking at the sky. The worst of the storm had passed and while the gusty wind was still strong, the rain had stopped, and bright sky began to peek through the dark clouds. The sound of thunder was now a distant echo.

"I take it our friends in the helicopter and boat are dead," the clerk said. He waited for a reply. When none came, he directed a question to the men who wore the traditional garb. "Where is Tammono?"

The men shrugged. One of them spoke up, "He was here when the storm started. He must have taken off when these devils arrived."

Walt could not put his finger on it, but he had a funny feeling something wasn't what it seemed. "You must be talking about the guy we laid out. Brock hit him with his gun and he was out cold when we entered the hut. When we came out he was gone."

"What's going on here?" Brock demanded. "Why did you deceive me and why are we here?"

The clerk exhaled a cloud of smoke. "You are here because these friends of yours," he said, gesturing toward Walt and Barb, "got too close to the Treasure of Oligand."

"What is that?" Brock asked, feigning innocence.

"Ha. Do not pretend to be ignorant of the Treasure. We know you found it."

"But what is this treasure? Why is it so meaningful?"

The clerk puffed on his cigarette, then squashed it out with his foot. "I will tell you the Legend of Oligand. You deserve to know since your lives will be sacrificed to appease the great God Oligand."

"Our lives will be sacrificed. You mean like human sacrifice? Geez," Brock said. "What year is this 1800?"

The clerk said, "You are close. The treasure arrived in these islands around the year 1712." He motioned to the circle of men standing around the clearing. "These men, along with myself, are the direct ancestors of the Tauri Tribe. In ancient times, our ancestors ruled these islands. They warred with other tribes, fished, built communities, and reproduced. Most of all, they lived free and the way man was meant to live.

This pleased the God of Life Oligand. For thousands of years Oligand watched over my ancestors and they prospered. Until one day, the white man appeared. The white man brought a scourge upon our people. He brought sickness and death. Within a few months an entire culture had been all but wiped out."

"You're talking about the Spanish Captain, Juan Carrera," Barb said.

The desk clerk had come across as a jovial man until Barb spoke up. His expression changed, and his face took on a malevolent look that sent shivers down her spine. When he spoke, his voice betrayed a vengeful tone of hatred. "Do not as much as mention his name in my presence. If you do so again, I will shoot you where you stand."

The clerk lit another cigarette and seemed to gather himself. When he spoke again, his voice returned to its former cordial tone. "So, the white visitors destroyed most of our ancestry and the Tauri Tribe never recovered. Since our brave brothers who were in the helicopter and speedboat are surely dead, the few men you see here are the only direct descendants of those ancient people and all that remains of our heritage."

Walt had remained silent throughout the conversation. He spoke up and asked, "You have a vast treasure at your disposal. Money can buy many things such as medical care and education. Why hasn't your tribe put the treasure to good use? Everything points to your story being true. There's no doubt your tribe can lay claim to the entire treasure. Why not use it for the good of your people?"

"The so-called treasure is poison," the clerk spat. "It is the reason for the demise of our people. When the white men arrived, the sickness began. Our people were dying by the dozens. Despite the actions of our Shamans, everyday brought new sorrow for the families of the Tauri Tribe. None of the prayers or sacrifices worked. Eventually, it came down to only one option. The white men had to die.

"One night, the remaining warriors who had not died off boarded the Spanish ship. They dealt death to the interlopers saving only the Captain and a handful of officers. These men were offered as a sacrifice to Oligand. The treasure was taken to the island, and also given as an offering. Soon, the sickness ceased. The great God Oligand had been appeased, but the treasure must never be removed, or the curse will return. As the few remaining members of our tribe, we vow to uphold the sacred treaty between ourselves and our Gods."

Brock snorted. "You can't be serious. The Spanish brought the disease and it went away after they were gone. By then, the disease had run its course. The same thing happened over and over throughout history all over the world."

In a vicious tone, the clerk said, "I am serious. What do you know of our people? You are nothing but another interloper." His gaze moved from Brock to Walt, then Barb. "You are all the same. You come here to our home, our rightful territory and presume to know what is best for our people. You will burn at the stake. We will see how knowledgeable you are when the fire licks at your feet."

Brock laughed. "You're nuttier than a fruitcake."

One of the men slammed the butt of his rifle into the back of Brock's head, knocking him to the ground.

"Take them inside and get them ready," the clerk ordered. He motioned to one of the other men. "You, get the fire started. We will pay tribute to Oligand tonight!"

Two men pulled Brock to his feet with rough hands. Brock used his weight to his advantage and forced the men to lift dead weight. Once he stood before them, he smiled and said, "Thanks boys. Now, if you'd be so nice as to carry me inside, I'd like to retire for the evening."

One of the men delivered a body shot to Brock's midsection. In typical Brock McGowen fashion, he laughed hard as though he'd just heard the funniest joke in the world.

Walt and the others were shoved and prodded into the same hut where Barb had been held. The men were stripped of their shirts and shoes, but left with their pants.

"They must have run out of island wear," Walt said.

Brock swayed his hips. "Damn, I was hoping to hula."

Two guards kept an eye on them with rifles at the ready. The others went outside to help with the preparations.

Walt looked at Barb and said, "Sorry, we almost rescued you."

Barb showed a warm smile. "Don't fret. If I'm going to be burned at the stake, I couldn't think of two better men to be by my side."

"I could think of lots of better men," Brock joked. Making a show of staring at the crude bandage wrapped around her thigh, he said, "By the way Barb, I heard you got shot."

"Not this again," Barb said in an exasperated tone.

"So, it's true. You got shot! Well . . . it doesn't surprise me; what with your habit of getting shot everywhere you go."

Barb chuckled. "I don't get shot everywhere I go. As a matter of fact, I don't get shot as often as you."

"You get shot more than me."

"You always get hurt. Look at you, you're hurt now. You have a swollen lip and a black eye already."

"Yea, but you got shot."

Walt spoke up, "It's not going to matter. If we don't figure out how to get out of here, we won't be worrying about minor injuries." Walt had reached the point where he was ready to attempt jumping the guards and using their weapons on the rest of the men. He figured it was better than being burned alive.

Brock said, "Yea, I have no desire to be sacrificed over a fire."

One of the guards overheard their conversation. With contempt in his voice, he said, "You will be sacrificed, unless you want to try to escape right now." He waved the barrel of the gun in their direction. "Go ahead, try to escape." When no one moved, he continued, "Have it your way. You will be burned alive and you deserve it. My brother was in the speedboat sent out to intercept you. His death is on your hands and you will pay for it with your own lives."

Brock replied, "His blood is on your hands. You're following an imaginary God and people are dying for no reason."

Walt knew it was a mistake for any of them to provoke their captives. The guard made a move toward Brock, but Walt stepped in front of the man and said, "All right, that's it. Burn us at the stake if that will appease your God."

The man never looked at Walt, but continued to stare hard at Brock. Walt knew it wouldn't take much to push the man over the edge. After a tense moment, the guard lowered his weapon and backed down. He took a step backward and stood beside the other guard by the door.

"I will rejoice when I hear your screams of agony."

22

_____

"They should have called by now," Claire said.

Mitch knew she was right. "I agree. Something must be wrong."

The storm had passed, but the sky remained partly cloudy and a rough chop roiled the surface of the ocean. The *Sea Spray* stood off four hundred yards from the atoll with only the main sail flying. Claire brought her stare to bear on her husband as he stood at the helm. "What do you want to do?"

"We have an injured man below deck, two young kids aboard, and no weapons. I don't know how much we can do." Mitch thought for a moment before going on. "We can start by circling the atoll. We'll stay close enough to keep an eye on things, but far enough away so we won't draw unwanted attention. Maybe I can slip unnoticed onto the atoll later, if we don't hear from them."

"That's not much of a plan."

Mitch shook his head. "No, it's not, but it's all I can come up with right now."

"We need help, real help. I think if we don't hear from

Walt within the next half hour, we should get the authorities out here."

"Who would we call?"

"We'll start with the police. If they have a Coast Guard, we'll call them. I don't know . . . the Navy. We can't sit around and do nothing."

"You're right, as usual. A half hour it is. If we don't hear anything we'll start making calls." Mitch turned the wheel and steered the boat for the far tip of the atoll.

"Time's up," the desk clerk said.

He stood in the doorway of the hut and motioned to the two guards watching the prisoners. The guards used their guns to prod the captives toward the door. Brock went first, followed by Barb with Walt bringing up the rear. A deep fear started to blossom in Walt's chest. He feared the time to move may have passed. They had no way of escaping now with two armed guards pointing rifles at them.

Passing through the door, Walt saw a blazing fire and the other men standing around. These men also pointed their weapons at the captives. Walt decided he wasn't going to allow this to go any farther. Instead of allowing these murderous heathens to burn him alive, he'd go down fighting. He stepped up beside Barb and stared in her eyes for a lingering moment. When he smiled at her, she returned a warm, understanding smile.

The next instant Walt turned his attention to Brock. "Well, old pal," he called as the group was forced toward the waiting flames.

"What's up?"

"You know what they say."

Brock laughed. "What do they say?"

"They say, you gotta die of something." As the words left his mouth, he reached for the gun the closest man held. Grabbing the weapon by the barrel, Walt jerked it from his hands.

Brock picked up on what Walt was hinting at and he moved just as fast, throwing a right cross to the back of the other guard's head. The blow knocked the man forward where he landed flat on his face. Walt and Brock had fought together through more than one scrape over the course of their lives and each knew what to expect from the other.

Barb was a different story. While she had escaped several life-and-death adventures, she didn't have the same hand-to-hand experience as the other men. That's why it came as a surprise when she used her leg to sweep the desk clerk's legs out from under him. He went down like a skater who lost an edge, landing on his backside. For a moment, Walt thought it looked as though they had a chance. Four more guards stood in the clearing, however, and they were all armed.

One of the guards opened up on Walt sending a row of bullets tearing up the sand at his feet. Before he had time to react, another volley blasted the sand in front and around his side. The guards were tough, hardened islanders, but they weren't military men. Instead of aiming the weapon, the young man merely pointed it in Walt's direction and yanked on the trigger. The result was hot lead flying wild. One of the bullets slammed into the guard who Walt had struggled with for the rifle incapacitating the man. With bullets zipping by his head, he had to abandon the rifle. Unarmed, he dove to the ground and rolled behind the relative safety of the corner of the hut.

Brock struggled with the man he'd knocked to the

ground. He finally wrested the automatic weapon from the man's hands, but he was too late. Another one of the guards unleashed a three-shot volley. One of the slugs hit Brock high in the shoulder. The tremendous force of the slug drove Brock back and knocked him off his feet. He landed on his back with a grunt.

Barb came to her feet after taking the desk clerk down. When she saw Brock get hit, she stopped and stared in horror. The moment of hesitation cost her as the clerk got to his feet, pulled a pistol, and placed it against her head.

Walt saw the events unfold. Even though he was pinned down, he vowed to help. He had to do something. Just as he came to his feet, he caught a movement at the edge of the clearing. A man stepped out holding a primitive bow like the one Ricardo Baez had used to shoot Walt. Walt recognized the man as the guard he'd knocked unconscious earlier, the same man who had disappeared while they were freeing Barb.

He wore the traditional garb and when he raised the bow, Walt thought he looked like something out of an old encyclopedia depicting ancient island tribes. Before anyone else noticed, the man aimed and fired the bow, releasing a feather tipped arrow that flew straight and true. Unlike the arrow that hit Walt in the thigh, this arrow flew with much more speed. The razor tipped shaft sliced into the desk clerk's back.

The clerk froze in shock as the arrow hit him. He lowered the gun and turned to see what had happened. The man with the bow didn't hesitate. He nocked another arrow and shot the closest guard in the chest. The man stumbled and fell to his knees.

While everyone turned their attention to the man with the bow, Walt made his move. Crouching low, he dashed for the man who the guard had shot. He was sprawled out on the ground writhing in pain and trying to get to his feet. The rifle lay next to him in the sand. Walt could smell the coppery scent of blood as he knelt and brought the gun to his shoulder in one smooth movement.

Barb saw the opportunity and slammed her fist down on the clerk's wrist. He dropped the handgun, but didn't pay much attention to Barb. His eyes were wide, and he reached around to his back in a feeble attempt to remove the arrow buried deep in his abdomen.

Walt leveled the rifle on the man who had shot at him and yelled out, "Hold it! Everyone just stop!"

Barb bent down and picked up the handgun. The man with the bow nocked another arrow. The remaining guards stood with their rifles ready but at least the shooting stopped.

The clerk finally stopped groping for the arrow in his back and said in a cracking voice not much louder than a whisper, "Troy. What have you done?"

The man with the bow replied, "I am doing what should have been done long ago. I am putting an end to this madness."

"But you are one of us. You are a Tauri."

"Tell the rest to lower their weapons. This ends now."

The clerk glanced around. He understood the situation had slipped from his control. "Do as he says, brothers. We will live to fight another day."

The men did as they were told. Walt wasn't sure who this man was or why he saved their lives, but he decided it wasn't important right now. Brock was down with a gunshot wound and that was the pressing matter at hand.

He used the business end of the rifle to gesture to the

clerk and his men. "You men line up over here where I can keep an eye on you. Barb, can you have a look at Brock?"

Barb nodded and knelt beside her injured friend. "Well, Brock, it looks like we're even in the getting shot department on this trip."

Brock was only half-conscious. She had seen bullet wounds before and even took a bullet to the leg, but this injury was different. Although she joked, Barb saw the seriousness of this wound. The bullet entered high on Brock's chest and exited directly through his shoulder blade. The bright red blood indicated he suffered severe damage including a probable injury to his lung.

"Hang in there, old pal," she said. Turning to Walt she pleaded, "He needs immediate medical attention. If he doesn't get it, he'll die."

Walt stared hard at the man with the bow, sizing him up. "What's the fastest way back to Tahiti?"

"We came in a small speed boat," the man answered, lowering his bow without nocking another arrow.

"That's no good," Barb said. "It would be too much bouncing around."

"What happened to our phone?" Walt asked the man.

"They destroyed it as soon as they took you into captivity."

"We'll have to get in touch with the Hathaways," Walt told Barb. "They have communications with the outside world."

Walt thought for a moment, then decided. "I know it's not ideal, but we're going to have to put Brock on the speedboat and get him out to the Hathaways. They have communications and very good medical supplies. It's his only chance."

"OK, let's hurry. The faster he can get medical treatment, the better his chances are."

Walt addressed the man with the bow, "I don't know who you are, but we could use your help to get our friend to the boat."

"I have a Tauri name, but my real name is Troy Narmand. Of course I'll help. Wait here," the man said.

He ducked into the closest hut and came out a few seconds later with a handful of plastic wire ties. "Here, use these," he said, handing half to Walt. Together, they bound the tribesmen's hands behind their backs.

When Troy got to the clerk, the man voiced his displeasure. "You will pay for this, you traitor."

"You will pay for the men you've killed, including my father. I know you were on the boat."

"Ha! You know nothing."

"Do not fear. The arrows are not poison tipped. You should survive," Troy said, ignoring the statement and pulling the ties extra tight.

When they finished, Walt motioned to where Brock lay. He knelt and lifted Brock's shoulders and head. Troy carried his legs. Together, they struggled along the path, but eventually made their way to the beach and the boat, which turned out to be the boat the men had stolen from Brock. Barb followed with the Hathaways' handgun and the shotgun. She left the rest of the weapons behind. With as much finesse as they could manage, they lifted Brock aboard the speedboat. Barb climbed up the ladder at the stern and as soon as she was aboard Walt fired the engine and drove the boat away from the beach.

Rounding the Southern end of the atoll, Walt searched in vain for the *Sea Spray*. "They're not here!" he cried in an exasperated tone.

"Relax," Barb said in a steady tone. "They can't be far."

Giving the engine more gas, Walt powered the boat around the side of the atoll where they had come ashore. As he rounded the Northern tip, the billowing white sails of the Hathaways' boat came into view. He heard Brock groan but ignored it and gunned the engine. Barb wove frantically as they neared the sailboat.

By the time Walt eased the boat alongside the *Sea Spray*, Mitch, Claire and both kids waited at the rail, ready to help. With a combined effort, Brock was taken aboard, and he soon rested below deck in one of the children's bunks. Denny occupied the other child's bunk. Claire and Lynn seemed to have the most medical experience, and together they disinfected and bandaged Brock's entrance and exit wounds and did everything they could to keep him comfortable. He had not spoken since he received the gunshot wound.

"Poor bugger's lung is collapsed," Claire said. "His chest is filling up with air. We need to do something to relieve the pressure."

Lynn noticed a grim frown on Claire's face. "What can we do?"

"We need to take the pressure off his chest. Hand me the hypodermic needle and syringe please."

As Claire positioned the needle on the end of the syringe, Lynn stared through frightened eyes. "You're not going to do what I think you are with that . . . are you?"

"I've had a bit of medical training during my boat racing career. This is extremely risky, but I don't know any other way."

"No offense, but a Doctor should perform this procedure."

Claire stared Lynn in the eye. "No offense taken, mate.

Your friend does not have time. We have to relieve the pressure right now."

Lynn had worked fishing boats her entire life. No stranger to gruesome wounds, she had seen everything from broken bones to hooks impaled in people's faces. "Trust me, Claire, I'm not squeamish. Brock's a dear friend and his life is on the line." After a brief hesitation, she said, "Do what must be done."

Claire gave her a sincere nod. "Just try to hold him steady. I'm not sure how he'll react to this."

When Lynn had Brock's arms pinned down, Claire raised the needle and inhaled a deep breath. "One, two, three."

On the count of three, she plunged the needle into Brock's chest slightly above his top rib.

Brock shuddered for a second, but that was all. In his current condition, he could not respond. Claire drew back on the syringe and immediately heard the sound of air filling the plastic tube.

Exhaling a relieved breath, she said, "I think it's working."

Lynn continued applying weight, effectively pinning Brock while Claire drew air from his chest cavity. At last the syringe was full. Brock showed instant signs of improvement. He breathed easier and when Claire checked his pulse, his heart rate increased to a more normal pace.

Claire said, "Whew! It actually worked."

Lynn raised an eyebrow.

Claire shrugged and smiled. Both women broke into nervous laughter. They knew they were on shaky ground and both women felt relief at the outcome.

"This is a temporary fix. He needs proper medical attention, but I think he's stable for now," Claire said.

23

W alt secured Brock's boat to the stern of the *Sea Spray*. When he got up on the deck of the sail boat, he faced the man who had wielded the bow. "OK, so who are you?"

"My name is Troy Narmand," the man replied. "I am a member of the Tauri tribe."

"You shot your own people. If you are Tauri, why did you help us?"

With a scowl on his face he said, "Those men are fools. They follow an ancient law that is nothing more than superstition. Meanwhile a treasure lays buried, and my people go without proper food, medical attention, and education."

"So, you stood against them."

"I have always been against them. When I was a child, my father spoke out against what they were doing. He wanted to move forward and bring my tribe into the Twentieth Century. Many, many nights I heard him arguing with the other men of the tribe while they sat by the fire. Even though I was a very young boy, my father used to discuss some of what was said at these gatherings. He said he might not be able to persuade the others to go along with his ideas although he would never stop trying to convince them of the mistakes they were making. My father said if he could not change the Tauri ways in his lifetime, I should continue on until they stop this madness. He made me promise I would never stop fighting for my people and never allow the evil men to win. Today I fulfilled that promise."

Barb stood to the side, listening. "There were so many things the ancient people didn't understand. Lunar eclipses, earthquakes, they had no way of knowing what was going on."

"That's right," Troy said. "But now, things are different. Believing in old curses is not the way to protect our people. The Spanish brought disease to our people. Now, the great treasure that they brought can be a blessing."

"So where does Ricardo Baez fit into all of this?" Walt asked.

"Ah, Ricardo Baez, my old friend. I was a young boy when he arrived. It was not long after the elders of the tribe killed my father. Oh, I know they did it. All these years they do not suspect I know, but I do know. I have no hard evidence, or I would have brought it forward to the authorities.

"They said it was a boating accident, but three men went out fishing and only two of them came back. My father was the strongest swimmer of the three. He would have made it to safety before the other two. Besides, I overheard the elders talking a few days before the incident. One of them mentioned something about how they would get rid of my father. The other man agreed. I told my father and he said he would be careful, but I think he knew it was inevitable. He was one man against many.

"Anyway, about six months after his death, Ricardo Baez

showed up on his boat. He started snooping around, looking for the Spanish treasure. So, of course, the Tauri tribe has to do what it has always done. When word got out, the elders gathered and started making plans, the same way they did when you started snooping around.

Walt and Barb glanced at each other before Barb said, "They were watching us from the very beginning."

"Yes, of course. Instead of building good lives for their families, that is what Tauri tribesmen do. In the case of Ricardo Baez, the men captured the crew and sank the boat on the reef of the small atoll where you found Ricardo."

Walt said, "That was the wreck I found when we first got here."

"Yes. The tribesmen were supposed to capture all of the Americans, but Ricardo escaped. The tribe spent three days searching until they finally caught him. When they did, he was brought back here," Troy gestured toward the atoll, "and readied for sacrifice."

"Just like they were going to do to us," Barb said, fighting off a shiver.

Troy nodded. "Isn't that a useless thing to do? Imagine throwing away people's lives for nothing."

Walt snorted. "If you look at the world around us, this type of thing goes on all the time. Think about all the lives wasted over pleasing a God."

"Well, I witnessed the murder of Ricardo Baez' crew. The men of my tribe tied them to poles and built fires at their feet. I was so shocked I felt immobile at first, but soon I remembered my father's words. I remembered what they did to him and I vowed not to allow it to continue.

Ricardo was to be sacrificed the next night. That afternoon when no one was paying attention to a young boy, I sneaked to the hut where they held him. I freed Ricardo and led him to where I had a raft waiting.

Before he could get far enough away, the men discovered he was gone and set out after him. He made it as far as the atoll where the treasure is buried before they could catch him. Members of my tribe will not step onto that atoll because of the curse."

"The men from the helicopter didn't have a problem stepping on the atoll," Walt said, gingerly touching the spot where the slug slammed the stock of the gun into his head.

"Those men are not Tauri. They are paid help . . . mercenaries. The last of those men went down in the helicopter crash. Tauri tribesmen will not set foot on the atoll where the treasure is buried. Ricardo Baez knew this fact and used it to survive for all these years."

"Until I killed him," Walt said, feeling a pang of guilt.

"You must not blame yourself. When I helped him escape, he was a sane man. For the first few years, his main focus was survival. I used to bring him supplies every few months just to keep him alive. However, the effects of living alone on an isolated atoll in a remote part of the Pacific took its toll. After a few years he no longer merely fought for survival. His focus went to the treasure. He became possessive and even long after the tribal men had forgotten about him, he would not leave. He traveled back and forth between atolls, but he never desired to leave the area. He could not abandon his coveted treasure. Over the years, I believe Ricardo Baez went insane."

"That explains a great deal," Walt said.

"Just as I helped him escape the madness of the Tauri tribe, I have now helped you and your friends. You must go. Do not stay and go insane the way Ricardo did. Go and tell the world what has happened here. Maybe what's left of my tribe will be able to put the treasure to good use at last."

Barb stared toward the atoll. "That's going to be hard to do."

Walt and Troy followed her gaze. Three men on a speed-boat were skipping over the waves, heading straight for them. Even from this long distance, they could see the clerk sitting in the bow cradling a rifle.

Turning his attention to Mitch, Walt said, "You might want to reload your weapons, I think the bad guys escaped their bindings. No one thought to bring the automatic rifles and it looks as though we'll be outgunned."

Mitch spoke to his son. "Go below and get your mother. You stay down there and take care of your sister." He motioned to Brianna. "Go on, honey, go down with Andrew and stay there until me or your mother says it's all right to come up. Understand?"

"Yes, Dad."

When Claire reached the deck, Mitch handed the wheel over and grabbed the ammunition. "Steer to starboard and we'll try to hold them off for as long as we can," he told his wife.

He handed the box of shotgun shells to Walt and began to load the nine-millimeter handgun himself. Both men crept to the port rail with weapons loaded.

"I have an idea," Walt said, watching the speedboat come closer. "Maybe I can get to the other boat tied to the stern, the cabin cruiser. That boat's faster and turns sharper than the *Sea Spray*. I'll be able to maneuver better plus we'll have two boats to their one."

"Good idea. I'll give you cover until you can untie it and get away."

Walt sprinted to the stern.

The speedboat turned to parallel the sailboat. As soon as it did, the man in the middle seat opened fire with the rifle. Walt felt his anger rise at the thought of bullets flying toward a civilian vessel with children on board. The first shots went high. The man adjusted his aim and four fountains of water erupted as his shots hit the water just in front of the hull.

In one smooth motion, Walt climbed over the stern rail and dropped onto the forward deck of the cabin cruiser. This left him exposed and he hurried to crawl back to the cockpit of the boat. As he did, one of the attackers noticed him. The man at the tiller backed off on the throttle and the boat fell back toward the stern of the *Sea Spray*. The clerk and the man in the middle seat began to fire simultaneously. Mitch got off a few rounds and the speedboat swerved away but not before several shots hit the cabin cruiser. One of the slugs tore into a fuel line and a spark from another ignited the fuel. The next instant, a bright orange ball of flame erupted from the engine compartment under the rear deck. Along with black smoke, the flames billowed toward the sky. Walt was thrown to the deck, but other than scuffed knees and elbows, he was uninjured.

The stern of the cabin cruiser began to sink, and Walt knew his plan would not work. He had to get back aboard the *Sea Spray*. In quick succession, Walt got off two shots. The speedboat was out of effective range for the shotgun, but the act of someone shooting at him made the man at the tiller slow and swerve a little farther away from the sailboat.

Using the distraction, Walt clambered up on the front deck and sprinted for the bow. Reaching the very tip of the boat, he tossed the shotgun over the rail of the sail boat and leapt. Walt didn't make the deck, but he landed against the stern. He hung onto the rail with everything he had, gathered his wits and strength, and climbed over the rail and back aboard the *Sea Spray*.

The attackers were shooting again, and Mitch provided cover by firing back. Walt saw two neat holes appear in the mainsail as shots went high.

At the same time, Claire turned the wheel hard to starboard. Huge waves of spray fell over the deck as the boat responded to her manipulations. This maneuver put the speedboat almost directly behind the larger sailing vessel. The turn should have put a good deal of distance between the boats, but the sinking cabin cruiser was slowing the *Sea Spray* down and affecting her maneuverability. Claire pointed to a shelf beside the wheel and shouted, "Walt, you have to cut the cabin cruiser free she's dragging us down! Here, use this knife!"

Keeping his head down, Walt grabbed the knife from its sheath on the shelf and ran to the stern rail. He used a sawing motion and quickly cut through the painter fastening the boats together.

Opening the throttle, the man at the tiller brought the boat back to the port side and began to pull alongside once again. Mitch worked his way along the rail almost to the stern. He steadied the handgun on the rail and squeezed off three shots.

The shots missed, but weren't totally ineffective. Again, the speedboat slowed and swerved away. The man in the middle seat rattled off a few shots, Mitch fired back. The situation had turned into a deadly running gunfight on the rising and falling swells of the South Pacific. Occasionally, Walt aimed and fired the shotgun, but usually the distance was too far, so he held off, saving his ammunition. The clerk jumped into the action and soon two men shot at the *Sea Spray*. Mitch was a good shot, but he was outgunned. One handgun was no match for two automatic rifles. Sooner or later a bullet from the rifles would connect with someone aboard. Splinters of fiberglass burst up as three slugs tore across the deck.

Claire worked wonders keeping the boat facing away from the deadly rifle fire. Every time the speedboat pulled parallel, she turned away providing much less of a target to the pursuers. Walt crouched and crept to the helm where he found Troy hiding behind the bulkhead of the cabin.

"Mitch, come here for a second, I have an idea," Walt called.

24

Mitch ran to the helm. While he reloaded his gun, he cracked a wan smile. "I hope it's better than your last idea," he said only half-joking. "We can't hold out much longer."

"Troy has a bow and I have a shotgun, but the range is too far. The next time it gets parallel to us, I want Claire to turn toward the speedboat instead of away from it. When she does, we'll all be able to use our weapons."

Mitch nodded.

Walt looked at Troy. "Are you up for it?"

Troy nodded. "I am. I think it's a good plan. I have three arrows left and I don't want to die with any of them still in my quiver."

Walt turned his attention to Claire. "As soon as we get a round of shots off, turn away again so they don't get much of a chance to return fire."

"Got it," Claire said through gritted teeth.

A bullet hit the main mast ricocheting away and splintering a piece off the side as the speedboat again paralleled the *Sea Spray* on her port side.

"Ready!" Walt yelled.

Claire spun the wheel and turned the bow of the boat toward their pursuers. At the same time, the three men hurried to the port rail. In unison, they rose, aimed, and fired. Walt saw the surprise on the faces of the men in the speedboat. Without hesitation, he pulled the trigger and the gun kicked and he lost sight of the men for an instant. He heard more shooting as Mitch began to fire. Shouts came from the smaller boat and the next time Walt got a look at the men, he could see the man in the middle slouched over clutching his shoulder. The man at the tiller turned the boat and goosed the throttle in an attempt to put some distance between himself and the suddenly dangerous sail boat. Bullets from Mitch's nine-millimeter tore up the water around the boat. An arrow sailed just over the man's head. Walt pulled the trigger, pumped the action of the shotgun, and pulled the trigger again. When he paused to look, the boat was motoring directly away, skipping over the waves. He felt the sailboat lurch as Claire turned toward starboard and the opposite direction from their attackers.

Walt met Mitch's gaze. Both men smiled. Then, he heard a grunt. Troy stood on unsteady legs. A river of dark blood ran from a large bullet hole in his chest. With determined eyes, he stared at Walt and Mitch and declared, "We did it. I did it. I have fulfilled my father's wishes." With that, he stumbled sideways and crumpled to the deck. In the instant it took for Walt to kneel over the islander, he had stopped breathing.

Mitch knelt beside Walt and said, "He died saving us."

Walt nodded. "He was a very unselfish man . . . a true hero. I'll make sure he is treated as such. And, I'll make sure his family, if he has one, is well taken care of. I'll make sure those responsible pay for what they've done." As Walt finished speaking, he glanced toward the speedboat and turned with a jerk. The attackers were coming back.

Walt and Mitch secured Troy's body, so it wouldn't fall overboard, then rushed to the port rail.

"Turn to starboard," Mitch called to Claire. "They're coming back."

In the bow of the speedboat, the clerk had his rifle pointed in their direction. Walt could see blood around the man's head and neck. He knew he must have caught him with the shotgun blast. It was obvious the man at the tiller had also suffered injuries. He operated the motor with his right hand while favoring the left, which was covered in blood. The man in the center of the boat lay across the seat face down. His condition was unclear, but it did not look as though he posed much of a risk.

Mitch started firing as the boat drew near. When he emptied his gun, he knelt and began to reload. Bullets filled the air as the clerk fired wild shots from the bow, then the *Sea Spray* was turning again. Claire maneuvered the boat, so the gunman didn't have much of a target. Walt slipped a few more shotgun shells into the magazine. "We're going to have to come up with a different plan. This isn't working."

Just then, Claire yelled, "Look!" She pointed to the East.

Walt and Mitch followed her pointing finger and saw a helicopter coming in their direction. Unlike the helicopter that had harassed them earlier, this helicopter had pontoons for landing gear enabling the craft to land on the sea. Across the burnt-orange fuselage, the words COAST GUARD were painted in black. When the helicopter circled, Walt saw the pilot and the two-man crew clearly. The men in the other boat saw them too. They immediately broke off the chase, turned and headed back toward the atoll. The helicopter continued to circle, and Mitch went below. A minute later he came back on deck with a hand-held radio. Dialing into the emergency channel, Mitch established communication with the Coast Guard.

Claire turned into the wind. Walt helped Mitch furl the sails and stop the boat. When the *Sea Spray* drifted dead in the water, the helicopter hovered overhead. A crewman rode a cable down to the deck. Next, a basket was lowered from the hovering helicopter. The men unclasped the basket from the cable, took it below and loaded Brock onto the metal-framed stretcher. When they brought Brock on deck, the crewman secured him in the basket and gave a signal to the other crewman. This man used a winch to recover the basket. Within ten minutes of the arrival of the helicopter, Brock was speeding on his way to a hospital.

The crewman who boarded the boat stayed aboard for the return trip to Tahiti. He remained in communication with his base and when Claire brought the boat into a slip in the harbor, a full detachment of Coast Guard personnel was waiting to help Denny. Lynn went along with Denny to the hospital, as did the remains of Troy. The remaining survivors aboard the sailboat were escorted to police headquarters to give accounts of what happened. Two Coast Guard members stayed aboard the *Sea Spray* as guards.

The Hathaways finished giving their accounts of the day and were released from police questioning at nine-thirty that night. They gathered up their tired children and took a taxi back to the *Sea Spray*.

Walt and Barb received medical treatment for the arrow and gunshot wounds they had received. The doctor gave each a good prognosis and signed their release. They were taken from the hospital straight to questioning at the police station. They didn't see the outside of the police station until well after midnight.

From there, they went right to the hospital to check on Brock's condition. Due to the late hour, there were no doctors on duty. Despite Barb's relentless questioning and stern tone, a lone nurse at the charge desk relayed vague information about Brock's condition. She didn't go into much detail and would notspeculate about his chances for survival. All Walt and Barb knew for sure was that Brock had been in surgery for over four hours and was currently bedded in the Intensive Care Unit. A doctor would be available for conversing on Brock's condition in the morning. Since they already had a room reserved and couldn't do anything to help Brock, Walt and Barb retired for a restful night in comfort at their hotel.

Eight o'clock in the morning found them back at the Center Hospitalier Territorial Hospital. Lynn had spent the night in Denny's room. Walt and Barb checked in with them first and found Denny doing fine. He was awake and alert. The doctors said he had suffered a concussion and a broken ankle. The concussion should not have long-lasting effects, but the ankle was a different story. He had suffered a bad break and would need months of rehabilitation. He probably wouldn't even walk without crutches for over a month.

While his diagnosis and prognosis weren't ideal, Denny felt good to be alive.

"The odds of surviving a plane crash aren't that great," he said, "And Lynn came out of the ordeal without more than a scratch." The fact that his wife and unborn child were fine did wonders to lift his spirits.

More good news waited when Walt and Barb went to the I.C.U. to see Brock. The doctor who performed the surgery was at the desk signing papers and going over some charts. When Barb inquired on Brock's condition at the desk, he spoke up. While Brock's condition remained serious, he was out of immediate danger. The doctor told Walt and Barb that the situation could have been much different if not for the fast thinking and actions of those who administered aid on the boat. Brock shouldn't be moved, and he would have to be closely monitored to ensure he didn't develop infection, but barring a setback, he should recover fully within a short time.

An antiseptic smell permeated the room when Walt and Barb entered. They sat by his bed listening to the steady sound of breathing for a few hours. There was no way of knowing if Brock realized they were there, but staying by his side felt like a show of support and the right thing to do.

———

The police and Coast Guard were active with the first light of morning. By evening, they had the three remaining Tauri tribesmen in custody. With the help of a local anthropologist, the cave was excavated, and the treasure cataloged and removed. The centuries-old manifest and journals were examined in great detail over the next several weeks. As a team of experts worked to piece the fantastic tale together, a clear understanding of how the treasure ended up in the Society Islands developed.

The journal and paperwork from the Spanish ship along with local legends passed down from one generation to the next showed a voyage of dreams ending in tragedy. In the year 1712, the Spanish brought enormous riches out of the Bolivian and Chilean jungles. Thousands of indigenous people were forced into labor to transport the gold from mines deep in the rugged South American interior. The Spanish loaded the treasure onto ships at the port of Valdivia. On July twentieth, a fleet of eight ships departed for Spain with their cargo of gold and silver. The Spanish ship Octavio, had been held up for three months for repairs. Finally, on October nineteenth, she set sail for her return trip to her homeland.

However, the Captain and crew had different ideas. Tired of the harsh conditions and lured by tales of friendly island people, the Octavio sailed for the Society Islands. Whether the Captain ever planned on returning to Spain or not is unknown, but the ship did make it to Tahiti and the surrounding islands.

The Doctors deemed Denny Smith healthy enough to be released from the hospital the next morning. Although he was not cleared for travel by the authorities, Denny felt grateful to be alive and able to spend time with his wife and friends in a relaxing setting. A plaster cast encased his ankle and would remain for at least six weeks, but Denny considered that a minor inconvenience.

"I only got shot so you wouldn't feel like a loser Barb," were the first words Brock spoke when he finally woke, late the next afternoon.

With Walt, Barb, Denny, and Lynn by his side, the rough and tumble former mining engineer from the Midwest forced a weak smile.

Barb returned the smile and leaned down to place a kiss on his cheek. "As long as you're in my life, Brock McGowen, I'll never feel like a loser."

Even in his weakened condition, the color returned to his face.

Walt said, "Look, you made him blush."

"Don't fool yourself, Ulrich, the woman wasn't born who could make me blush."

Walt laughed. "Is that right?"

Before Brock could reply, Barb spoke up, "I might know one woman who would disagree, and she's on her way here at this very moment."

This time, the red flush of Brock's face left little doubt. He blushed in earnest and said, "Martha?"

Barb nodded. "She's on a flight over the Pacific as we speak, courtesy of Seven Seas."

Walt grinned and squeezed Barb's arm. Pride swelled in his heart. He felt fortunate to have Barb in his life.

25

As the sun set on the western horizon, Walt and Barb joined the Hathaways for dinner aboard the *Sea Spray*. Claire fixed an Australian casserole called Old Fashioned Fish Pie.

As Walt, Barb, Mitch, and Claire, along with their two children enjoyed the meal, they discussed the events of the past few days. They talked about the different members of the Seven Seas team and how it would be impossible to replace any one of them. They also talked about Troy Armand, the young man who gave his life helping others. Barb announced she would place a plaque on the wall of honor in the Kendall Outdoors headquarters. The name and story of Troy Armand would take a place beside the name and story of Art Kendall on the wall of honor for people to see for all time.

Barb also let it be known that people like the Hathaways meant the world to her. Like Walt, she valued true friends more than any monetary rewards life offered. And like Walt, she loved her life even if she felt as though she was living on the edge sometimes.

Mitch and Claire earnestly liked Barb also. As the four adventurers exchanged conversation, Walt took particular interest in the children. Andy and Bri behaved in a far different manner than most children of similar age. Considering what they had witnessed in the waters off the small Pacific atolls, they acted as though the whole ordeal was just another of life's adventures. Walt joked back and forth with the well-traveled youngsters.

From the corner of his eye, Walt noticed Barb studying him. When he glanced at her, he saw a faint grin and a strange look in her eye. After a long moment, her gaze went to the kids. Not wanting his hosts to catch on to what he sensed, Walt broke the moment by tossing a piece of fish to Shooter, who gobbled it up in one bite with tail wagging.

On the walk back to their hotel, Barb said, "Good food, good wine, and good friends . . . what a lovely night."

Walt agreed. "The Hathaways are a top-notch couple and they do a great job raising their kids."

When Walt took a casual look at Barb, he saw the strange look in her eye again.

"What?' he asked.

"Mmm, I don't know. Nothing."

Walt felt frustrated by Barb's unfamiliar reaction. "Are you all right?'

Barb stopped walking and stood face to face with Walt. "I'm fine, Walt," she said with a warm smile. "Everything is fine."

They continued strolling toward the hotel when Barb said in a coy voice, "Do you ever think about having children?"

Walt finally understood.

"Sure, sometimes. I mean, I haven't in a long time. You know . . ."

"Relax, Walt," Barb said. "I am not telling you I want to have your children. But, I do think you'd make a wonderful father."

"Ha! Sometimes I can hardly take care of myself, never mind kids."

There it was again. Barb's eyes wore the strange expression once again. "You're alright, Walt. As a matter of fact, you're pretty near perfect."

Walt wrapped Barb in his arms and kissed her.

At that very moment, Denny Smith felt his wife stir by his side in their hotel room bed. He placed his hand on Lynn's belly and felt their unborn child move.

Brock McGowen snored softly in his hospital bed. He dreamed about Martha Brown and beer. A thin smile creased his lips.

Mitch and Claire Hathaway tucked their kids into their berths on the boat and smiled at each other, thankful for what they had.

Walt broke off the kiss and held Barb tight in his arms.

She stared in his eyes and said, "I felt so scared and alone when I thought you'd been shot and killed. I'm so glad you're alive."

"I can say the same thing about you. Although I would never stop searching for you, I wasn't sure I'd ever see you again."

They embraced and stayed in each other's arms for a long while.

THE END

ABOUT THE AUTHOR

Keith Dissinger was born and raised in the United States. He currently lives with his wife Anne in Western Canada where he works in the oil fields and writes Adventure novels.

You can keep up to date with new releases through my website or sign up for my spam free newsletter for the latest news on my books.

www.keithdissinger.com

Thank you for reading ATOLL, I truly appreciate it. Word of mouth is pivotal to the life of a book, it helps readers decide if the book is for them. I would appreciate it very much if you would leave a review.

CHOOSER OF THE FALLEN

My next book is called **Chooser of the Fallen**. Here is a short sample of the opening of the book.

The icy grip of the water leeched through the tough fabric of the wet suit and chilled the man's skin. He did not allow it to bother him, he grew up on the shores of Ireland and had long ago become accustomed to frigid water. Moving his head in an upward motion, he used the forehead mounted dive lamp to scan the hull of the boat directly overhead.

The man wasted little time. He moved toward the stern and used his gloved hands to stop his progress and steady himself against the hull. In the inky black water, he felt around in his dive bag until he found what he wanted. Working with precise movements, he attached a packet of plastic explosive to the hull. He set the timer, gave the deadly device one quick look over, and stroked away.

The man passed under three more boats before quietly surfacing at a wooden ladder. From the shelter offered by two moored boats, he slinked up the ladder and surveyed the deserted dock. When he felt certain he could cross the planked dock without detection, he rose and crept to the far end where his truck was parked. Shadows blanketed the area. The man had broken the bare bulb on the light pole earlier. With smooth movements, he changed out of the wet suit and into the garb worn by the local fishermen; dark, heavy trousers, a long-sleeved shirt, and a wool sweater. Leather boots covered his feet.

With the scuba gear thrown in the back of his truck, he slid behind the wheel and started the engine. As he drove away from the dock, he said a silent prayer for the lives that would be lost on the unforgiving sea in the morning.

The alarm on Janice Brown's phone sounded at four a.m. She reached out and fumbled with the screen as the alarm grew progressively louder. At last, she shut the alarm off, brushed hair from her eyes, and stepped out of bed.

Her current assignment covering cod fishermen as they plied their trade in the rough waters off the Norwegian coast required early rises. As a field reporter for Seven Seas Television, the twenty-two-year-oldwas accustomed to early mornings and working unconventional hours. Just a few months ago, she'd been working nearly around the clock in Morocco. Placing her phone on speaker mode, she pushed the number for Ted, her cameraman, and began to get dressed for the day.

When Janice heard Ted answer on the third ring, she said, "I'm up. Are you ready?"

His voice sounded groggy, "Yep, wide awake."

"Good, I'll meet you downstairs in five minutes."

Twenty minutes later, Ted strode through the front door of the hotel to find Janice waiting under the eave. A fine, misty rain fell, and thick fog shrouded the old building.

The hour of day, nor the weather, hindered Janice's sunny outlook on life. "Good morning Ted. Did you sleep well?"

The thirty-year-old African American carried a box of video equipment in each hand. Although he wasn't a morning person, he loved his work and felt blessed to have a career with Seven Seas. He stared at Janice through bleary eyes, then cracked into his infectious smile and said, "The bed was hard and the mattress too soft. We're not in Kansas anymore Dorothy. But, never mind, I'm ready to spend a day at sea."

Right on cue, the hosts for the day pulled up in an old half-ton truck. The driver got out and held the door for Janice. "Good morning friends. Are you prepared for some fishing?"

Janice flashed a smile. "Absolutely. We're looking forward to observing some real life, hardworking fishermen."

A second man helped Ted load the gear onto the floor in the rear of the truck. "Good morning."

"Good morning to you sir."

When everyone was situated in the truck, they started for the docks. As the truck jostled along the dirt road, the morning fog hid the beauty of the Norwegian fjords. Janice felt slighted. She'd arrived the previous evening and hadn't had a chance to admire the architecture of the quaint fishing village.

Following a short drive, they arrived at the boat and began to get things squared away for a day of fishing.

The Captain spoke while he worked, "We are going to have heavy seas today. You sure you won't get seasick?"

Ted looked offended. "I've never been seasick a day in my life."

When the gruff captain snorted, Janice said, "I don't think you'll have to worry about us, we'll be fine. Is there anything else we can do to help?"

The captain, a seasoned veteran of many years working the inhospitable North Atlantic waters, furled his brow. Deep cracks formed in his leathery face when he smiled. He admired their spunk, even if he didn't believe they were as infallible as they let on. "Well, all right then. Let's finish stowing the gear. Afterward, you can help cut bait."

Janice and Ted threw in and helped ready the *LADY,* a thirty-five-foot fishing vessel built in 1972. Gear was stowed, nets were inspected, and pumps, winches, and pulleys prepped for hard use. With an hour to go before daylight, the *LADY* chugged through the harbor and out to open sea.

A gusty breeze blew across the deck and light rain pelted the crew. Once the boat cleared the sharp point sheltering the harbor, she encountered an angry sea sporting six-foot swells. Janice felt the thrill of adventure as the hardy boat rode the waves like a broke pony. She also felt a tinge of fear as the captain guided the boat out to sea. Had she known the timer on the packet of plastic explosives fastened to the *LADY'S* hull ticked ever closer to detonation, her fear may have been paralyzing.

MORE BOOKS IN THE SEVEN SEAS ADVENTURE SERIES

THE PACT

HOTEL CALIFORNIA

OCEANS OF AFRICA